EMBER FALLS

The Green Ember: Book II

EMBER FALLS

S. D. Smith

Illustrated by Zach Franzen

Story Warren Books

Trade Paperback edition ISBN: 978-0-9964368-0-9
Hardcover Edition ISBN: 978-0-9964368-1-6
Also available in eBook and Audiobook.

Story Warren Books,
an imprint of
Brightener Books
www.brightenerbooks.com

Cover and interior illustrations by Zach Franzen, www.atozach.com.

Map created by Will Smith and Zach Franzen.

Printed in the United States of America.
16 17 18 19 20   01 02 03 04 05
Manufactured by Thomson-Shore, Dexter, MI (USA); RMA12JM384, July, 2016

Story Warren Books
www.storywarren.com

For Gina

Nunc scio qui sit amor, salutem in arduis esse.
Vivat crescat floreat!

Village Green
Community Garden
Helmer's Tree
Village
Caves
Plateau
Maggie's Porch

Rockback Valley

Cloud Mountain

Halfwind Citadel

To Jupiter's Crossing

PROLOGUE

How am I going to die?" Prince Lander asked. "Will I be carried off by those monsters?"

"I don't know, Your Highness," Massie said. "But it's better to live as you will want to have lived, rather than spend your time worrying about the end. You are right here in your story. Don't skip ahead." Massie stood alongside the young prince on the prow of *Vanguard*, scouting the increasingly turbulent river for perils.

"Lieutenant Massie, would you call me 'shipmate' and not 'Your Highness'? After all, we're in the same company," Prince Lander said, pointing to the black star patch on his shoulder.

"We are shipmates, sure. But you're also my prince. I'm afraid I can't pretend you're not. You must be a prince, and I must be your loyal servant."

"I suppose so," the young prince said, frowning.

"What's troubling you? Have you had those dreams again?"

"Of being carried off?" Lander sighed. "Yes. I'm always

afraid something bad will happen."

"I'm sorry to hear that, sir. The memory of Seddleton is still fresh," Massie said, peering into the distance with a scowl. "Now I'm growing afraid myself—afraid of this poor visibility. I can't see well enough in this growing fog."

"I can still see *Burnley's* mast there, two—no, three!—points off the starboard bow. She still has her sails set," Lander said. "She should hail if there's danger, should she not?"

"Aye, but Captain Grimble doesn't always hail us with great haste. Please pass the word for Captain Walters. Say that I beg he will take in sail. Say we cannot see well enough to scout."

"Aye, sir!" Lander said, and he scurried off.

Massie kept at his vigil as fog swept over the boat. He could see almost nothing now, and he turned back to peer through the gathering mist on deck. The ship was not yet slowing.

"On deck there!" he shouted at a passing sailor. "Hayes! Go and wake the king."

"The king?" Hayes asked.

"Aye, the king," Massie said. He swerved through coiled ropes and sailors at their stations. "Captain Walters?" he called. The deck was dense with fog. There was no response. "Commander Tagg!" No answer.

He found the bell rope and rang it hard. "All hands, take in sail! Heave to and drop anchor. Where's the officer of the watch? Find Captain Walters and Commander

Tagg!" He heard calls and answers, the sounds of sailors stumbling through the fog.

King Whitson appeared on deck in his nightshirt, rubbing at his eyes. Just then a rending crack sounded and the ship grounded to a halt, spilling all hands forward. Pained groans and harried cries accompanied the grinding churn of wood pressing against rock.

"Boathooks!" Whitson called above the clamor. He rose slowly, with a wince, from the deck. "Deploy boathooks and get us off that rock! Master Owen, take a lamp and check the hold. I have no doubt we are sprung. Start the pumps."

"Aye, sir!"

"Hamp!" Whitson shouted to a hurrying sailor.

"Aye, Your Majesty?"

"Please go below and beg the queen to come on deck."

"Aye, sir!"

"Carry on, bucks!" the king shouted above the buzzing din on deck. "We must save our ship! Remember what precious cargo we carry."

"It's too late, Your Majesty!" Massie shouted, panting as he ran up. "I've been over the side. *Vanguard* is wrecked. It's only a matter of time—"

Before he could finish explaining, the ship lurched and began sinking rapidly.

"Where is *Burnley*?" Whitson asked. "Can anyone see her sails?"

"There's no sign of her, sir," Massie said. "And they don't answer hails."

"They never warned us, neither," Prince Lander said, joining his father.

"Launch all boats," Whitson called. "Start the mothers and children over first, then every doe. Massie, you go. Lead them to shore."

"Aye, sir," Massie said, then hurried through the press of active sailors. "Make a lane! All boats overboard!"

Hamp reappeared, looking nervous.

"What is it, Hamp?" the king asked.

"It's the queen, Your Majesty," he said, swallowing hard. "Queen Lillie is gone."

"Gone?" Whitson asked. "Gone where?"

"By Flint's own sword," Lander said, eyes wide and terrified. "She's carried off."

from *The Wreck and Rise of Whitson Mariner*

Chapter One

A Mission

Picket Longtreader moved through the fog, uncertain which way to turn. He was careful to be quiet. The enemy might be lurking just beyond the bank of mist ahead.

He hoped they were.

Picket could only faintly make out the swish and tap of his companion's deft steps. Smalls, the prince, was with him. And Picket was with the prince, heart and soul.

The fear was there, familiar and clear. Picket inhaled, acknowledging its presence while at the same time assigning it a place of service. It would have to sharpen his mind. Fear would not, could not, be his master. Not today. There was too much at stake.

His parents needed him. His brother, Jacks, needed him. Picket hoped this was his chance to free some, or all, of them. If any were still alive. He swallowed hard and hurried on.

After another minute, he sensed that the prince had stopped moving. He felt a touch through the fog. Smalls appeared beside him, out of the mist, a worried look on his face. He bent close to Picket's ear and whispered, "This is a perfect place to keep slaves for their mine: deep in this valley, near the river, in the foothills of the High Bleaks. But we should have heard them long ago. I haven't heard one shout or the rattle of a single chain. Have you?"

"Nothing," Picket answered. He was worried that Smalls would want to stop, to return to the main force a mile back, where Lord Victor Blackstar and Captain Helmer waited with a regiment of soldiers capable of liberating the slaves they'd been assured were here. "I want to go on."

"I'm not sure that makes a lot of tactical sense," Smalls said.

Picket knew he was right. Especially with the prince himself present. But Smalls had insisted on personally accompanying his friend on this mission. He said that honor demanded it. Now that they were here, Picket didn't want to turn back.

"It's my family," Picket said, a catch in his voice. He thought of Heather, his sister and closest friend. He remembered the hopeful look on her face when she said goodbye to him a few days before. "Heather's counting on us." They *had* to be here.

Smalls nodded reluctantly. "We can't do this alone, Picket," he said. "We observe. We report back. We're only scouting. Do you understand?"

"Yes, Your Highness," Picket said, bowing his head quickly.

They moved forward, Smalls rubbing at his eyes. Picket considered for a moment the weight that must press on his friend. Smalls had been revealed as Jupiter's heir, had triumphed in a strategic battle, and now served as the open leader of the cause and an object of hope to rabbits across Natalia. Saving the prince, as Picket had done so heroically at Jupiter's Crossing, had been easy compared to the task before Smalls now.

A resistance to unite. An impossible foe to conquer. A kingdom to win.

The Lords of Prey were great birds, an ancient alliance of raptors that had haunted the rabbits of Natalia since Whitson Mariner first touched land with his wandering community. From their home in the High Bleaks, they had frequently attacked rabbits throughout the Great Wood, and beyond. Whitson's heirs all fought them, but only King Jupiter had truly driven them back.

Jupiter's heroic victories had ushered in an era of flourishing unlike any in history. But that golden age ended when he was betrayed by Garten Longtreader, Picket and Heather's uncle, and delivered over to Morbin Blackhawk. King Jupiter was killed and the kingdom was lost. Morbin and his Lords of Prey, allied with wicked wolves under the command of Redeye Garlackson, burned and fouled vast swaths of the Great Wood.

Some rabbits gave in to the new order, but many more went into hiding or joined the secret citadels, an uneasy alliance against Morbin's forces. King Jupiter's heir, revealed to be Heather and Picket's friend Smalls, achieved a crucial victory at Jupiter's Crossing. But the task remained enormous and the cause fragile. Visions of the Mended Wood sometimes felt like a hopeless, happy dream, destined to be dashed to ashes in an awful waking moment.

The fog hung thick and the ground fell away as Picket and Smalls descended from the foothills into the rocky valley below. They could now hear running water. Picket saw white fog before and above him, dark stone beneath his feet. Apart from a whispering wind, the faint water flow, and their footsteps, it was quiet. Too quiet.

Picket was just about to suggest that they head back and report when he heard a faint thrashing borne along on the wind. He couldn't tell where it came from. Picket expected Smalls to stop, but the prince moved forward, quickening his pace. Picket followed.

Smalls reached for his sword, and Picket drew his own. He hadn't used it in earnest since he flew over Jupiter's Crossing and put an end to Redeye Garlackson. He was ready to use it again, if he had to, to free his family from their cruel captors.

The fog began to clear, and Picket caught a glimpse of what they had been hearing. A river. More shapes were coming into view, but Smalls pointed urgently to the back of a small wooden hovel. They dove behind it as the fog thinned.

Smalls motioned for Picket to wait while he peered around the corner of the beat-up shed. The prince looked long and hard while Picket leaned against the brittle wall, his sword at the ready. Smalls finally turned back, a puzzled expression on his face. He shook his head. There was nothing moving. He nodded to the other corner of the shed.

Picket slid into position and slowly edged an eye beyond the wooden wall. Hopeful only moments before, he now watched as curtains of mist rose and fell in the strengthening wind and the scene was revealed. He saw a soot-stained hillside cave, apparently an abandoned mine. He saw the river, a rotting dock propped on its rocky bank, and a large collection of hovels like the one they hid behind. Nothing else. No one else. The mining camp, a riverside collection of dingy broken-down sheds, appeared deserted.

He frowned, and Smalls sighed. Picket felt his excitement and battle dread drain away, turned to bitter disappointment. He felt hollow, suddenly weak and cold. He hated the idea of returning to Heather with nothing and seeing her face when he told her he had failed to bring their family back. His muttering moan was lost in the wind.

Then another sound came, loud, urgent, and angry, arresting his reverie and sending a wild surge of panic through his body. Smalls cried out as Picket spun around and looked up.

Three massive birds of prey swooped down on them, talons flashing, hideous shrieks pouring from their razor beaks.

Chapter Two

THE CHASE

Picket froze for a moment, but Smalls never hesitated. He broke through the fragile wall of the hovel, dragging Picket inside just as the foremost bird struck, slicing past in a terrifying flight. The two other raptors landed behind and tore into the shed with their talons. But Smalls and Picket were already barreling out the front door and running for their lives along the stony bank.

"Stay sharp!" Smalls shouted. Picket scanned the shoreline as his feet pounded the ground, his vision bouncing in the wild panic of their flight. No boats. No signs of life. Nothing but this endless row of broken-down sheds. They raced past the mine site, choosing not to enter and risk being trapped.

Picket glanced back, fearful of the frenzied shrieks and beating wings that grew louder and louder. The birds were airborne again, bearing down on the two fleeing rabbits. Picket felt as vulnerable as he ever had. Terror filled him, and he ran harder, catching up with Smalls, whose wide eyes darted all around as he sped on.

They weaved between buildings to elude the pursuit. Most were small hovels like those they had first encountered, but occasionally they hurried past a larger, longer, sturdier building. They ran hard, a thin sliver of hope pushing them on. Backward glances told Picket their weaving escape was buying precious time but wouldn't save them. One of the birds had gone aloft, calling out to the others, who pursued them along the ground, flying expertly between the sheds, gaining on the rabbits every second.

"They're on us!" Picket said.

"Follow me!" Smalls shouted. Instead of dodging around the next building in their path—one of the large, longer ones—Smalls plowed into it, once again breaking through the wooden wall. Picket followed, crashing through behind Smalls, and the two rabbits rolled onto the wide floor among shards of wood. The nearest bird beat his wings in a halt outside and clawed at them through the broken wall. The hole wasn't large enough for the bird to enter, but Picket felt a vicious slash across his back as he rolled into the first of many wooden support columns. He turned and drew his sword, and both rabbits slashed wildly at the flashing talons.

The rest of the wall was shredded in seconds by the three attacking raptors, and soon their enemies were inside. What had seemed a large room became a death trap as the massive birds filled it, breaking everything in pursuit of the two rabbits. Picket's ears rang with their horrible shrieks, their frenzied advance making strategy impossible.

18

Picket jumped back, staggered up, ran, and stumbled backward. Several columns lined the middle of the building, and the birds smashed through them as they came. Picket swung wildly with his sword, never knowing what he might be striking. He ended up on his back near the far wall, pain and wild rage a fire in his mind as he watched a raptor coil and strike, tearing through a third column in his race to finish Picket off forever.

Picket found his feet and dove backward, through the far door, rolling onto the hard stone as the building collapsed on the attacking birds, sending a plume of dust and debris into the air and momentarily obscuring the enemy.

Picket searched frantically for Smalls. When he saw him only a few feet from the wreckage, he hurried toward him. The strong young rabbit had come through somehow. Picket gasped with relief. Smalls struggled to stand and picked up his sword, his weary arm dragging the tip along the stones. Picket reached for his own sword, but it wasn't there. He turned to face the rubble alongside the prince.

The dust cloud settled, and the only sounds were the gasping breaths of the two battered rabbits. They inhaled, bending, trying to recover and make sense of their escape. An eerie silence filled the valley. Finally, Picket smiled.

"Your Highness, that was—" he began. But he was cut short when the ground shook, the rubble rumbled, and a bird's head appeared through the debris. With a terrific leap the raptor broke free of the ruined building, scattering tattered sections of the wreckage. Shaking his wide wings, he rose above the rabbits with a horrifying screech.

Picket's eyes widened, and a cry died in his throat. Terrified, he glanced at Smalls. Smalls set his feet, raised his sword, and gave a defiant shout.

Chapter Three

IMPOSSIBLE WAR

What Picket saw next, he couldn't immediately explain. As he ran forward, swordless, toward the rising raptor, the sky filled with light. Fire, in fact. Picket didn't understand. He stopped, blinked, and turned to the prince. Smalls was smiling. Then it began to make sense.

Arrows. Flaming arrows streaked ahead against a background of darkening grey sky.

He heard cries, the voices of their reinforcements. Thirty flaming arrows found the already wounded bird and sent him spiraling into the river. He would not rise to fly again.

Picket crossed to Smalls, still terrified at the thought of losing the prince. Lord Victor Blackstar ran in, with Captain Helmer at his side, surrounded by ready archers and soldiers with swords drawn.

"Any others?" Helmer asked, breathing hard.

"I don't think so," Picket said. "Two in the rubble, but most likely dead."

"Check the rubble and scout the perimeter," Lord

Blackstar called to a lieutenant, "and see if these are all we have to deal with."

"How did you know?" Picket asked, still gasping.

"One of our scouts saw a bird high up, headed your way," Lord Blackstar said. "We came fast and hard after that. I'm sorry we didn't get here sooner. Are you all right, Your Highness?"

"I'm fine, Blackstar," Smalls said. "Just disappointed to find the camp abandoned."

Picket looked around. He was glad to be alive, gladder still that the prince was going to be all right. But a deep disappointment settled on him. To come so far, only to fail! He groaned.

"What about you, Ladybug?" Helmer asked, bending to examine Picket's wounds. "Looks like you'll have a keepsake from today."

"I'm all right," he answered, wincing as Helmer wiped at the long gash. "It's just, I thought…"

"I'm sorry, lad," Lord Blackstar said. "I know this is a hard blow, not finding your family here. But stay on the job, son. Do the next right thing."

"What is next?" Picket asked, stooping to the ground and breathing deeply.

"A winter war against birds like these," Smalls said, indicating the two bodies his soldiers were examining in the wreckage.

"An impossible war," Helmer said, applying a field dressing to Picket's neck and back.

"A hard one," Lord Blackstar said.

"How can we fight a war against such creatures?" Picket asked. "It took forty of us to defeat one."

"Or," Lord Blackstar said, "it took two to defeat two."

"It was blind, crazy luck," Smalls said, shaking his head.

"He's right," Picket agreed.

"Then, Your Highness, we shall have to figure out how to be lucky more often. And we shall have to be blind to impossibilities," Lord Blackstar said. Then, laying a hand on Helmer's shoulder, he added, "I think we have the crazy part covered."

Chapter Four

HEATHER'S PLACE

Heather should have been happy. She had finally been approved as a doctor in training and had received the badge of her accomplishment, a medic satchel. Halfwind's version of a calling ceremony was different than Cloud Mountain's. This was a citadel of war but at the same time a place brimming with serious, even pious, devotion. Here, the votaries held a ritual for all guilds in Leapers Hall.

Heather loved the ceremony and felt pride in her calling. She had hopes of being assigned to assist Emma. Her friend, now a full doctor, led the team of healers at Halfwind Citadel. Emma had risen quickly in the medical ranks when an outbreak of blue fever at Harbone Citadel carried off many of the doctors who had come to help. She had gone there, done wonders, and survived, earning a reputation for bravery and excellence.

Heather herself had been widely celebrated as the Scribe of the Cause, a vital asset in the emerging war. Her account of the victory at Jupiter's Crossing, read and spread widely, had helped to galvanize the opposition to Morbin's Lords of Prey. She had purpose. She had a place. So why was she unhappy?

"Are you having those dreams again?" Emma asked as they walked the winding dirt-walled passages that served as Halfwind's secret citadel. "The vivid, troubling ones?"

"No," Heather answered. "Well, yes," she corrected. "I am still dreaming more and more. Yes. But that's not what's bothering me."

"You're thinking of your family," Emma said, laying her hand on Heather's shoulder. "You wish your parents could see what you've become."

"That's true," Heather said, dodging a hurrying soldier. "I'm pleased to be here with you, with Picket, and many of our friends. I'm grateful for how you've helped me in my training."

"But nothing can quite replace the part of you that needs to feel your father's arms around you, to hear your mother's reassuring voice again."

Heather nodded. "It's worse for Picket, I think. He acts brave, but he's hurting. I know it. Down deep. He was so helpless that day when the wolves came. He had to watch while our family was taken and our home burned. He's changed so much since then, and he wants to act! He hates doing normal things while they're still out there, enslaved— or worse. He's haunted by the promises he made to Jacks. Lord Ramnor's refusal to sanction another rescue attempt has him fuming."

"But you know Lord Ramnor is right, don't you?"

Emma asked, nodding to a blue-robed votary as he passed. They came to a section where three hallways merged beneath a series of ornate stone arches. They waited for a tutor to pass through with her small collection of young students.

"Of course," Heather said as they moved on. "He has so many rabbits to think of and great strategies to implement. But I sometimes feel like no one can understand this kind of pain. As much as I love Lord Ramnor, he doesn't understand what it's like to lose your family. He doesn't know what Picket and I are going through."

"Perhaps not," Emma said, looking down.

"What am I saying?" Heather said, shaking her head and grabbing Emma's hands. "Emma, you're so kind. You have felt that ache your whole life, dear friend. And here I am whining like the world's most unfortunate soul. I beg you to forgive me."

"Never apologize, dear," Emma said, nodding to another passing rabbit, this one a doctor on her team. "You knew your family, so it's far worse for you. I never knew my parents. I do feel the ache of longing, the missing place in my heart where my father's blessing should be. I wonder about my mother, think perhaps I would be a different kind of a rabbit—a better rabbit—were she around. But you had that, and you lost it. And it's okay to be sad."

"You sound like the great Scribe of the Cause, not me," Heather said, linking arms with Emma as they walked.

"And you sound like the great Babbler Without Pause," Emma answered, nudging Heather with her hip so that she almost collided with a passing soldier.

"Sorry!" Heather said, bursting into laughter.

The soldier spun and winked at Heather, bowed dramatically, then turned and continued on his way.

"With friends like you, Doctor Emma, Lord Lady Physician of Secret Citadels and Shover of Apprentices," Heather said, "who needs Morbin Blackhawk?"

"May Morbin melt in his nest!" Emma said, pretending to toast Heather's invisible glass with her own invisible glass.

"May he molt in his vest!" Heather replied.

"May he revolt in his rest!"

"May he be tolt he's a pest!"

They walked on until they came to Lord Ramnor's ready room. Heather stopped and looked through the open door. She saw a crackling fire beneath the huge painting of Flint and Fay, those noble parents of rabbitkind, and the citadel lord huddled over a map-strewn table. Lord Ramnor's face was haggard, consumed with worry. She knocked.

Lord Ramnor looked up, a weary smile replacing his anxious stare. "Please, Doctor Emma," he said, "and Miss Longtreader, come in."

"Sadly, Lord Ramnor, I cannot," Emma said, bowing slightly. "My duties bear me away. But I leave the fate of my apprentice to you. I would assign her a place in the farthest, smelliest army, if I were you. But I'm just a doctor, so you do what you think best, my lord."

Heather smiled. She knew that Emma had recommended that Lord Ramnor keep her here and assign her as her own assistant.

"I shall do my best to oblige you, Doctor."

With a playful flourish of her hand, Emma disappeared, and Heather walked into Lord Ramnor's room and crossed to the fire. She had grown very fond of Lord Ramnor. He shared her love of stories and had lent her volume after volume from his vast personal library. She put out her hands to the blaze, enjoying the heat after the drafty corridor. Winter loomed, and Heather felt its chilly fingers beginning to stretch out.

"I'll do anything for the cause," she said, not turning around. "I know Emma has recommended I stay with her, but I don't want special treatment."

"But you are a very famous rabbit, Heather," he said. "Scribe of the Cause and sister to Picket Longtreader, the bane of birds."

"The brain of birds, more likely," she said softly to herself, smiling. Then more loudly she said, "I am a doctor in training in the army of Prince Jupiter Smalls. I will go anywhere I'm asked to serve. I will do anything for the prince's good."

"That is reassuring. I don't think your brother is very satisfied with his assignment with the Fowlers," he said.

"He loves being in the Fowlers. But he is, lord, bothered that he hasn't been allowed to search for our family."

"By the Leapers, I am too," Lord Ramnor said, and he seemed to sag as he reached toward the fire, rubbing his hands together. "But I'm planning for a war, and those plans can't include losing our best assets in another futile effort to save a few slaves—however precious they are. If we did that for everyone in the same position, we wouldn't have an army. And besides that, what Helmer and Picket are doing is essential to our efforts."

Heather nodded. "Both of us know our duty," she said. "We accept that it's not our choice."

"I'm glad to hear that, Heather. Because I have decided to alter your assignment. You will not be an assistant to Doctor Emma in the hospital here."

Heather's eyes widened. Her talk of serving anywhere was sincere, but it shocked her that Lord Ramnor would be that bold. It was widely known that she was close to the prince, that her Uncle Wilfred was the prince's dearest ally and friend. So, while she was sad that she'd be separated from Emma, she admired Lord Ramnor's courage. "I'll go anywhere," she repeated.

"Don't worry, Heather. You'll stay here." He smiled. "I have assigned you to Captain Helmer's unit. You will be the Fowlers' field medic. You'll be attached to his team but still serve as a member of the Halfwind medical staff, under the leadership of Doctor Emma."

"So you have kept me near my brother," she said. "And also Emma."

"I've put you where I think you'll best serve the cause."

"Thank you, my lord. I will do my best."

He glanced at his desk, where Heather saw reports of soldiers and maps organized neatly beside a clay vase bearing a fresh bouquet of pale yellow flowers. His face grew sad again. Heather winced. *What a burden to assign all these souls to places where he knows they will face unthinkable danger.*

"It cannot be easy to command at a time like this," she said.

"It is easier, I think, than being a healer. As you no doubt can foresee," Lord Ramnor said, "we'll need an army of healers in this war."

"I do see it," Heather agreed. "Though I didn't like to think of it during my training."

"Nor I, ever. For some it's fuel for purpose. But I don't like to think that all these soldiers I'm training and sending out will be wrecked by what's ahead. That so many will come back and need all your art and effort to make them whole again. That is, if they come back at all. So many won't."

"But on the other side of it all," Heather said, "the Mended Wood."

"Yes, I suppose we must think so," he said, smiling weakly. He looked into the fire. "You know in tales, Heather, how you believe it will go badly, but it all turns out fine—better than fine—perfect? It's not like that in a real war. In real war there's betrayal, and the betrayers win. In real life you get old staring at a growing heap of unhappy endings."

"I am young, lord, but I've seen betrayal. I never thought Kyle was capable of what he did," she said, thinking back to her one-time friend whose betrayal of the prince had nearly lost them the war before it started. *If Smalls had died...* Her heart ached at the thought.

"What's strange is that this Kyle character didn't succeed," Lord Ramnor said. "At least not entirely."

"No," Heather said, smiling. "We had our moment."

"And you wrote very eloquently about it. Half the rabbits huddled in burned-out backwoods have hope because of you. 'Bear the flame,' you said. And your tale had a happy ending."

"I love a happy ending," Heather said. "Because I need hope."

"Yes," Lord Ramnor said. "And that's just what your tale has done for those loyal to the prince."

"Then I'm glad."

"But," Lord Ramnor said, stoking the fire. Sparks flew up as he drove in the poker like a sword thrust. "I hope it's well-placed. I'm afraid we will all be disappointed. We're still faced with—and I say this because you are no longer a child—an impossible war. It's a war we—well, Heather, we can't win."

"We don't have to win the war today, sir," Heather said. She hoped she looked braver than she felt. "We only have to win the next battle."

Chapter Five

SWEEN'S SONG

Morbin's lair smelled of bones and blood. The sight of his throne, a wretched nest fashioned with gemstones and golden bones, always made her sick. But Sween had no choice about being here. She was a slave now, and her horrible duty involved keeping this vile den, this dark heart of the black hawk's kingdom, clean. So she worked. Like her fellow rabbit slaves, she worked. Silent and invisible, she moved from task to task without a word. Sometimes an old song would bubble up in her mind, rise unbidden to her lips. But she would always, at the last moment, catch herself. She must keep her silence and keep her place. There were no songs in Morbin Blackhawk's lair. Only dim lights, dark corners, cruel councils, and, for her, a plague of heart, wasting away her hope.

Sween bent at the base of the hideous throne, scrubbing at stains whose origins she never wished to know. Again thoughts came unbidden. Some were memories of recent terrors, but good memories pushed their way in. Happy scenes came to mind, of her old home, their old happiness together. She smiled, almost forgetting what vile work she did. The song came calling again inside her, a little shaft of light in the darkness of her grave day. She almost hummed, but a sudden whoosh of wings behind her made her turn.

With a beat of his wings and a heavy rattle and scrape, Morbin settled on his throne. Sween gasped, horrified to be so close to him. She smothered a scream, recovered herself, scrubbed mechanically a few more times, then backed away, bowing her head as she retreated. She snuck one glance at Morbin, and it was enough to make her stumble.

He was so large, wide-winged, and angular of features. His inky black feathers gave way to a golden yellow around his face, and his beak was long and sharp and awful. His breastplate bore his sign, a sharp *M* with golden stars at its base, and his helm was set on one of many pikes that surrounded his hideous throne.

His weapon, famous for foul deeds over the decades, including the murder of King Jupiter the Great, was still firmly in his grip. It was a long black sickle rimmed in crimson. A bloody tool for an evil lord. She shuddered, bumped into another scraping servant, and hurried from the room.

Breathing hard and shaking terribly, Sween crumpled onto the dark hallway floor.

The song inside her was gone.

Chapter Six

FLIGHT OF THE FOWLERS

Picket was soaring. He released the swinging rope and glided through the air, unsheathing his sword in mid-flight. With two hands gripping the hilt, he plunged the blade into his target. Withdrawing his sword, he dropped to the earth, rolling expertly into a run. He caught another rope and ascended once again, releasing to soar, his arms stretched like wings, his sword arcing behind him. He land-ed on a long branch, where he sliced at two more false birds with pumpkin heads perched upon them.

"I know it's a new sword, but try to hit one or two of them cleanly, Ladybug." Captain Helmer leaned against a tree and scowled, chewing on a stick of celery. "Those pumpkin-headed 'birds' aren't fighting back. If you can't hit them dead center, then you'll miss enemies who actually move when you fight them."

Picket could hardly hear Helmer. He didn't have time to lose his concentration now anyway. His team was count-ing on him to lead the way. He glanced down at his new sword, a gift from Prince Jupiter Smalls. Its steel was forged

from the rare blackstone they had found at the abandoned mine site. The pommel bulged with a large circular seal. The seal's design of a flying rabbit had been adopted by his unit—the Fowlers—and now he wore a matching patch on his shoulder. He sheathed the blade in a scabbard strapped across his back.

As he dove for another rope, this one on the edge of his leaping range, he panicked. Picket swam in midair, arms flailing. At the last moment he stretched desperately and snagged the tip of the rope. Catching it fast, he swung down in a wide arc. He let go, landed on another limb, and sprinted across it, leaping over several obstacles in his path. Up. Down. Wild swinging leaps. Flips and turns. Tricky patterns and surprising obstacles. He was nearing the end of the course.

Seven swinging birds, wooden creations bristling with blades, descended at once. Helmer had added several. He was always mixing things up to keep them on their toes. Picket pressed forward.

Jo Shanks landed just behind him, on time as always, to deal with the left flank. His bow was off his shoulder and he had an arrow nocked in an instant. Perkinson swung in and landed on a branch just above, his sword bared and his eyes darting. They surged forward, dodging as they ran.

Nearly there.

The target loomed before them. They had never been this close. Helmer actually stopped chewing and walked forward, craning to see his team closing in on their goal.

"Charge in!" Picket cried, reaching over his shoulder to draw his blade from the scabbard on his back. He pointed it at the bright target on the high-perched fort. Then the first of the final seven birds was on him. He leapt and sliced it free of its rope. The rope snapped, and it plunged far below, causing Helmer to sidestep the shattering wreck.

Who's a ladybug now? Picket smiled, adjusting to face the next foe while Jo and Perkinson dealt with their own.

One breath. Perkinson sliced into a pumpkin head, spraying its juice across the heights, then kicked the bird away.

Another breath. Jo fired arrow after arrow into the target, ducking below a swooping bird and cutting loose another with a flawless sword thrust.

Another breath. Picket felt a new presence behind him, another teammate gliding in to perfect the attack, while he focused on the final obstacles. Three swooping enemies and an impregnable fortress. But not this time. This time they would take it down. He focused on his approach, preparing to vault over a wooden wolf bristling with blades.

He was struck hard from behind. "Ahh!" He fell forward, nearly colliding with the wooden wolf, then jerked back and, overbalancing, tumbled and fell. He was high up in the tree, so he panicked, grasping for anything he could reach. He snagged a branch, flipped wildly, and struck several other branches on the way down. He landed at Helmer's feet in an inelegant crash.

Helmer bent, checked him for injuries. "Are you okay, Picket?"

Picket nodded. "I think so." He looked up and watched each member of his team stumble in turn, failing to reach the target. Each one was knocked from the sky in a series of painful collisions. Heyward, whose graceless entry had spoiled the attack, fell hard in a nearby bramble.

Heather rushed in and pulled Heyward from the bush, checking him carefully for injuries. She made him stay down and then ran to each of the other rabbits, finally ending with Picket and Helmer, who stood scowling.

"It was closer than ever," Heather said. "Don't be too discouraged."

"Close won't do, Heather," Picket said. "You know that."

"I understand, Picket," she said, touching his arm. "But even Helmer's elite Fowlers can't be perfect."

"We can be more perfect than we are," Picket said. He couldn't keep from glancing at Heyward as the others approached.

"And we shall be," Helmer said, nodding. He rose slowly and crossed to where Heyward sat beneath a tree.

"Please do forgive me, Captain," Heyward said, rubbing his face. "I will be certain to do very much better next time."

"I'm sorry," Helmer said. "The stakes are too high right now. Every day we're closer to an attack. Every day we're closer to battles with wolves and birds of prey. What Picket did at Jupiter's Crossing, how he flew and fought, it was extraordinary. The ordinary rabbit won't be capable of anything like that. But sometimes, some will have to be."

"I understand that," Heyward said. "That's why I'm here. That's why I left my hedges to come to this brambly patch and train. That's why I care so very much about the Fowlers. If we can do what Picket did, we can turn a battle—"

"But it's not for everyone," Helmer interrupted.

"What do you mean?" Heyward asked, rising.

"You did well when you helped me design and build the Fowlers' course. I'm glad you came with us to Halfwind. But I have to tell you, Heyward, that you're not fit to be in this unit. The Fowlers must be the very best, rabbits of extraordinary courage and daring. I'm sorry, son."

"So, I'm out? I'm out of the Fowlers?"

"Yes."

Picket noticed that Heather was about to speak, so he gently put his hand on her arm. He shook his head, imploring. She frowned but stayed quiet beside him.

Heyward wiped at his eyes. He looked as if he would speak again, but he finally closed his mouth and nodded. He fingered the patch on his shoulder, and Helmer looked grave. The patch bore the same symbol as did the pommel of the sword Prince Jupiter had given to Picket. It was round and featured in its middle a leaping, sword-swinging rabbit, behind which were spread wide wings that might be a wild cape. Heyward tore the patch free and offered it to Captain Helmer.

"Please report to Captain Frye and ask for another assignment," Helmer said, taking the Fowlers' patch.

Heyward disappeared, head down, into a hedgerow path.

"That was hard, but necessary," Captain Helmer said. "Now, let's review—"

"Was it necessary to do in front of everyone?" Heather asked. She stormed off after Heyward.

Helmer scowled. "Whose idea was it to assign us a medic?"

"Lord Ramnor, I think," Picket said. "It was right after you asked him if you could try to destroy," he coughed, "I mean, *train* some of his most promising young soldiers."

"You believe you are promising?" Helmer asked.

"Perhaps we're the only ones mad enough to say yes to this assignment?" Perkinson said, rubbing his shoulder and smiling wide. "So, we have a kind of mad promise. And you are always promising us pain."

"No doubt Doctor Heather will be valuable in the field as you hopeless maniacs flit from tree to tree," Helmer said, his lip curling. "But till then, I'm stuck listening to her."

"She's saved my life once already," Jo Shanks said, "so I'll defend her to the end."

Picket nodded. "Me too."

"You don't need to protect her, you collection of witlings," Helmer said. "You need protection—from *me!*" And he launched into an attack on the three of them, knocking them down with subtle tricks and swift kicks.

Why, Picket thought as he struck the ground, *oh why did I not expect that?*

Chapter Seven

A Walk in the Brambles

Heather stomped into the thicket, coming alongside Heyward. "It's all right, friend," she said. "I'd be happy to ask them to give you another chance."

"No thank you, Heather," Heyward said, his head hanging. "The fact is, they're right. I'm not at all suited for the Fowlers. They will do great things, I have no doubt. They will fly, as Picket did at Jupiter's Crossing. And I will dream of hedges and homes, of bridges and dams, while the world burns down."

"You've always wanted things straight," Heather said. "And there are few things more crooked than war."

"I just wish I wasn't so useless," he said. "I know I could be very silly indeed about my hedges. I see that quite plainly now. But I knew my place at Cloud Mountain and felt I offered something of value to the community. You know, Heather, I even kept the hedges in the forsaken acres on the plateau behind the caves, where the old standing stones had become almost a ruin. I tended the grounds, and the few secluded brothers thanked me. Even if no one else seemed to notice, they did."

"You're not useless, and you will do your part, Heyward. We're all still trying to find our place in this warren."

"I hate this war. It's unmaking the world."

"Morbin is unmaking the world. The war is our only answer to his unmaking."

"I suppose so," he said.

"But it will not be so..." she began.

"Yes," he said, nodding. "Of course. That old song. I had almost forgotten."

She stopped and let him go on, and he disappeared around a brambly corner. She stood in the path between the Fowlers' course and the warren that was Halfwind Citadel, sadness burrowing into her soul. She reached for her necklace, a gift from the prince. Touching it sometimes swept away her sadness in a wave of hope. It was a simple charm, bearing the sign of a burning flame, and she loved it.

She had written those words, words that so many now clung to.

The Green Ember burns; the seed of the New World smolders.
Healing is on the horizon, but a fire comes first.
Bear the flame.

What a noise she had made with her tale! But it was quiet there, among the paths of grass with tangled thorns and brush for walls. In many places it formed a canopy, so the roads in and out of Halfwind were like a maze to the untrained. After many weeks of being here, she was finally learning her way around. It saddened her to see Heyward, who loved to keep hedges neat, wind through this untidy maze after such a blow.

She thought of home, not Cloud Mountain but Nick Hollow, where her parents and baby brother had been captured. Her memories were a weight, and she felt like buckling beneath all the sad, hard parts of her story. Of everyone's. *When will we be free?* There among the thorns, the Mended Wood felt like a far-off dream.

Then she heard her name, called softly from behind, and she turned to see Prince Jupiter Smalls approaching. The future king. The rabbit who had rescued her. Her dear friend. She wanted to hug him, but she let go of her necklace, bowed quickly, and waved. A bright smile replaced her pensive frown.

"Have I interrupted you?" he asked, returning her smile.

"Yes, you have," she said, "thankfully." He crossed to walk beside her, and they wandered slowly through the tangled paths, saying nothing for a little while.

They walked into a clearing, past a patch of grass where bucks only a little younger than Picket played a vigorous game of Bouncer. They watched as a brown buck punted the ball aloft, and, when it bounced, all of them piled in to snatch it in its rebounding arc. But only one could win it. The ball-winner, eyes wide as his fellows chased him, wound his way toward a circle in the grass, where he touched the ball down with an exultant shout. Then he was kicking the ball high once more, and the chase resumed.

Heather smiled. "I would like to play this game sometime."

"Picket tells me you are very fast," Smalls said as they walked on, rejoining the path that bent toward the citadel entrance.

"I used to beat him at an old game we called Starseek. But that was in Nick Hollow, what feels like ages ago."

"Rabbits our age should still be playing games," he said, a heaviness coming into his tone. "Not trying to unite an alliance against a slaving monster's forces."

"Is it true you are going to Kingston?"

"I'm afraid so," he said. "Lord Blackstar arrived today, and he's managed to arrange a meeting with all the remaining citadel lords who are holding out on...well, on recognizing me as king."

"Then of course you must go, Smalls—I mean, Your Highness," she said.

"Please," he said, "call me Smalls. It's how my best friends have known me these last few years."

"But my sinister spies have learned that your given name is Prince Smalden Joveson," she said. "Is that true?"

"I'm afraid so." He laughed. "It actually is. But if I'm crowned, I will be able to choose my ruling name."

"Have you decided what it will be?"

"No," he said. "There's too much to do to think of such things now."

"I'm eager for your coronation, Smalls. It will be such a happy day."

"I hope so. When the war is over and I'm crowned at the First Warren, I'll be able to do many things I wish I could do now."

"Yes," she said, looking down. They walked on, finally coming to a path that led to the entrance of the citadel.

"Heather, please come to a meeting in Lord Ramnor's rooms at sunset. And bring Picket. Even here there is a need for secrecy, and I need all my most trusted counselors and friends present."

"You can be assured, my prince, that I will be faithful."

He smiled, bowed slightly, and moved toward the gate. She took a deep breath and turned back toward the Fowlers' course. She stopped when she heard a noise behind her. Smalls raised his head. His hand found the hilt of his sword.

Footsteps. Pounding toward them. Just around the bend in the briar path. Panting. Wheezing. Urgent footfalls.

Smalls drew his sword and stepped in front of Heather.

Heather braced for an attack. Her heart was pounding.

Then, around the bend, Captain Frye appeared, wheezing and breathless.

"Oh, Captain," Smalls said, returning his sword to its sheath, "I thought it was an attack."

"It might—" Captain Frye panted, "be."

Chapter Eight

Fateful Decisions

Soon they were all in Lord Ramnor's ready room, spread around a large square table. Maps and other papers littered the table and nearby benches. The door was closed and guards were set. Heather felt conspicuous. Why were she and Picket present? Why wasn't Emma here? Why the Longtreader children? *Well, we aren't exactly children any more. But we're not lords or captains.*

The only other young rabbits present—other than Smalls—sat on either side of a silent Lord Victor Blackstar, who had just arrived. One of his companions was a beautiful coal-black doe and the other a black buck with a white patch who might be her twin. Both were around the same age as Heather and Picket. They were all silent.

Uncle Wilfred, Captain Helmer, Lord Rake, and Lord Ramnor were also seated at the table. Smalls paced apart, while Captain Frye summarized the intelligence just received from his scouts.

"We have no way to account for this," he said. Captain Frye's voice was deep and menacing, full of rattlings. "But there is an…well, an army encamped about a day's march from here."

"An army?" Uncle Wilfred asked, rising. "So close? How did they get here so fast? We've watched all the routes."

"Not this route," Lord Ramnor said. "This is from the southwest."

"Morbin has no assets there; we would have known," Lord Rake said, running his hand through the fur between his ears. "How could he have hidden an army of wolves in such a desolate place?"

"Not wolves," Captain Frye said. "Rabbits."

A wave of anxious gasps sounded through the room. Heather didn't understand. She started to ask one of the many questions that flooded her mind but remembered she had been invited by Smalls, and she thought it best if she just listened. She saw that Picket was also struggling to keep silent.

"How?" Smalls asked. "How is it possible?"

"Your Highness, we don't know," Lord Ramnor said. "Our scouts—and they are reliable—have tracked them for days and have only just now gotten word to us."

"Your scouts have been wrong before," Uncle Wilfred said, glancing at Picket and Heather. She looked down. He was alluding to the mistaken intelligence that sent Picket and Smalls, along with many others, on a fruitless rescue mission. Some Longtreaders were believed to have been there. But when the rescue team arrived, they were nowhere to be found.

Heather saw that Picket's hands were clenched in a fist. Just over his collar she could see the edge of the scar that still stood out on his back. A souvenir from that failed rescue.

"We're sure this time," Captain Frye said. "Gathering intelligence is my responsibility. My mistake with the mining camp was most unfortunate, tragic even. But this information stands on far more solid ground."

"You own the mistake, though the mistake wasn't your own," Prince Smalls said. "You're a good leader, Captain Frye. I take your word that this is reliable. The question remains. Who are these rabbits, and what are they doing marching on this place, prepared for battle?"

"That is the question, Your Highness," Lord Ramnor said, turning to the others. "As the prince says, they are fitted for battle, marching beneath a banner that is strange to us. It's a black field with silver stars. Our chief scout says they look bigger, stronger, more terrible than any rabbits he has ever seen."

"Tall, terrible rabbits from the southwest, marching beneath a banner of stars?" Lord Rake said, rubbing his head. "I cannot even begin to understand."

"We have to assume, I think," Uncle Wilfred said, "that they are in league with Morbin."

"Agreed," Smalls said. "What now?"

"We can make preparations here, moving our scouts and advance units southwest. It would leave us more vulnerable elsewhere, but I don't see that we have much

choice," Lord Ramnor said. "We will make our stand and bear the flame." He smiled at Heather.

"I could send word for reinforcements from Cloud Mountain," Lord Rake said. "But they might mean to attack there."

"What about Blackstone Citadel?" Captain Frye asked. "It's the next nearest."

"They are still very reluctant," Lord Rake said. "Lord Ronan might even see it as a trap. I'm ashamed to say that he still does not quite trust Wilfred; nor does he yet acknowledge the prince."

"We are hoping to see him in Kingston," Wilfred said, "to help him understand the truth. But at the moment we still have a few citadels holding out, and Blackstone is one of them."

"For now we should prepare here," Smalls said. "Send word to Blackstone to let them know what we know. We must treat them as allies. Lord Rake and Captain Helmer should return to Cloud Mountain and organize a defense. More catapults must be prepared on the plateau. Wilfred and I will stay and aid Halfwind."

Heads went down, mouths pursed, and brows furrowed. Lord Blackstar looked down and began to write something. Silence brewed, uncomfortable and long.

"May I speak, Your Highness?" Picket asked.

"Of course," the prince said, motioning for Picket to stand.

"Sir, I believe your counselors would all agree that you

must go on to the conference of lords at Kingston." Heather thought how hard this must be for Picket to say. He must know that it would make his hoped-for mission to find their family all but impossible.

"But I can't leave you all here in danger," Smalls said, glancing at Heather.

"You must," Heather said, rising quickly to stand beside her brother. "The citadels must be united. You have to persuade them to join you. If you are never king, then this will never end, and we'll fracture into a hundred helpless bands. I don't know who these tall rabbits are, or what they mean. But I know Morbin plans to thwart you, to ruin us all and make us his slaves." She pounded the table.

Lord Blackstar stopped writing and looked up, a smile forming on his stolid face. She stopped a moment, almost sat down. But she stood tall again and went on. "I want to be free! I want my king. You should go to Kingston, Smalls. Your Highness, go with Uncle Wilfred and Lord Blackstar. Forge an alliance that can bring an end to all this woe. If war comes to us while you're away, we will bear the flame for you."

"Yes, Your Highness," Picket said. "Heather's right. We will do whatever you command, all of us, to the end of the world. But you should go."

The prince looked down. "It is a hard thing to go to safety when you will be in peril."

"As you know, Your Highness, kings must do many hard things," Uncle Wilfred said.

Lord Victor Blackstar rose and spoke at last.

"If you will be king, an event on which hang all our hopes," he said, "you must go to Kingston and meet these errant lords. You will not, I assure you, be fleeing danger." He glanced at the two rabbits on either side of him. "Kingston was forged in war, and it lies in the southern foothills of the Low Bleaks. We live in Morbin's shadow. Our conference plots, beneath his nose, to depose him. It won't be easy."

The prince nodded gravely.

"Indeed," Lord Ramnor added. "There are no safe ways now."

"It's war," Helmer said. "All is hazard."

Smalls sighed. "As all my counselors agree, I will go. But I leave behind one very dear to me, who may succeed me if I fall."

At the words "one very dear to me," Heather's heart beat faster, but she was confused. *Succeed?*

Smalls looked at the three lords in turn, then last of all at Wilfred, a question in his eye. Each nodded.

"Then it is agreed," the prince said. "You shall all know our secret. It must go no further than this group. It is vital for both her safety and the good of the kingdom."

Picket looked as confused as Heather felt.

"There is one who will rise to rule if I fall, and it's vital that you all work to preserve her in our absence," he said, nodding to Lord Rake.

"Preserve who?" Picket asked.

"My sister."

Chapter Nine

THE SECRET PRINCESS

Heather stared at Smalls, shaking her head. *How can this be?*

"My sister," he went on, "has been protected by my father's friend for many years. She is unaware of who she is. We did this so she could live without the burden of constant peril that I have lived under. All of our other siblings have gone over to my oldest brother, Winslow, who rules at First Warren as a puppet governor for Morbin. They are slaves. She is free. And she has been free of that terrible choice. Therefore, the faithful lords have accepted her as the appointed heir should anything happen to me."

"She would be queen," Heather said, sadness surging through her.

"Yes," Smalls said, a sad smile on his face.

Heather felt like collapsing. She stumbled back, reaching for her chair, nearly knocking it over as she sat down heavily. She thought of her life at Nick Hollow, of all that had been kept from her while she lived there. She remembered how painful it had been to stand at Lighthall on

Cloud Mountain, surrounded by the ten windows showing past and future glories, and learn the truth about the
Longtreader family. She had centered her identity in the
hope the tenth window showed—Smalls crowned and ruling the Mended Wood. And now she felt the frayed threads
of her story begin to unravel again. Her head swam. Picket
sat beside her and took her hand.

"Who?" she heard Picket ask. She could not even raise
her head.

"It's Emma," Smalls said.

Heather looked up, a wave of relief washing over her so
suddenly that tears pooled in her eyes. Then, just as quickly,
it ebbed, replaced by a growing understanding of what this
would mean for her, and for her dearest friend.

"Emma is your sister?" Picket asked.

"Yes," Smalls said. "It is a great secret. No one else must
know that she's a princess. That she is *the* princess."

"Not even her?" Heather asked, looking intently at
Smalls. "You won't tell her even now that you're leaving?"

"No."

"But what if something happens to you?" Heather
asked, tears spilling from her eyes. "She should know. She
should hear it from you. She has wondered about her family
for years, and to think that she is a princess—that she has
a family! She has to know."

"On this I remain firm, Heather," the prince said. "She
has a family, yes, most of whom are traitors. I know what
it is to carry this burden. I know what it is to be hunted

and betrayed. I would do anything to spare her from what I have experienced."

"And it's more than that," Uncle Wilfred said. "It's for all of us. It makes sense as a tactic. If only a few of us know, then the chance that our enemies know is that much smaller. Since my brother Garten turned, betraying King Jupiter to his death, we have had an endless series of betrayals. None of us has to look very far. From Smalls' brothers to my brother, from Challabat to Kyle, traitors abound. Even King Jupiter's older brother, Bleston, would not acknowledge his brother as heir and left before his coronation. This world is teeming with traitors. It's the most effective of our enemies' methods."

"It is, sadly, only too true," Lord Ramnor said.

Heather was stunned. She felt pulled in many directions. Her devotion to Smalls, to Emma, and to the cause. It was a jumble of confused loyalties. Beneath it all was a river of relief sliding into an ocean of foreboding.

"Can I trust you to be faithful?" the prince asked.

"Yes," Picket said.

"Always," Heather said, but her heart grieved. Not because of who Emma was, or even because she must keep it secret. There was more. Now that she knew the contingency plan for what would happen if Smalls were killed, she felt a weight of woe settle on her heart. It was as if Smalls already had one foot in his grave.

A silence lingered, and only the crackle and hiss of the fire could be heard. Heather looked at the flames and longed for her lost home and her father's tales. She realized that she lived inside those tales now, but it brought her no joy.

"We must go at once," Uncle Wilfred said.

"Yes," Lord Blackstar agreed. "Ramnor, I leave my children with you. Assign them wherever you see fit."

"Very well, Victor," Lord Ramnor said. "I know what it means for you to leave them with us."

"They are accustomed to vigilance and are entirely trustworthy," Smalls said. "I have known them for many years. Heather and Picket, I'm so sorry. In all this I have forgotten to introduce you. I'd like you to meet Coleden and Heyna Blackstar, old friends of mine from my rambling exile. We have had some adventures," he said, laughing.

"We are due some more, it seems," Coleden said, smiling. His sister was silent, but she smiled at the prince too. She was strikingly beautiful, her fur black and shimmering and her air one of confidence and grace. She seemed like someone out of a story.

Heather did not like her.

"May I suggest you consider leaving Heyna to be with Emma?" Lord Blackstar said. "She has been trained to fight and could serve as a last line of defense to protect the princess."

Heather started to object, feeling protective of her dearest friend, but she trusted Lord Blackstar and Lord Ramnor. She tried to silence her nagging doubts.

"Certainly," Lord Ramnor said, nodding to the prince. "And Coleden?"

"I have an idea," Helmer said. "As of today we are short one Fowler."

"He would be an excellent choice," Smalls said.

"We must go, sir," Uncle Wilfred said.

"Yes," Lord Blackstar replied, hugging his children and whispering in their ears. They nodded gravely and smiled at their father. Heather winced, a great pain of heart seizing her. She looked over at Smalls, and he met her gaze.

"I am sorry to be leaving," he said. "Very sorry." Then everyone was looking to him, and he addressed them all. "Thank you, friends, for your faithfulness. We are beset by many dangers, and traitors multiply in the dark. It will not be so in the Mended Wood."

"In the Mended Wood!" everyone repeated, though the words were more solemn than cheerful.

"I am grateful for you—each of you. We go, but we will return. Look for us when hope is almost gone. And always, for the sake of this wounded world," he said, looking at Heather with a sad smile, "bear the flame."

Chapter Ten

GIVE ME YOUR SWORD

Picket watched Heather go and, after a moment's pause, followed after her.

"Picket, wait," Smalls said, crossing the room. "Can we speak privately?" Picket nodded, and they crossed into an adjoining room. Once inside, Smalls rubbed his face and sat down heavily on an old couch. "Listen, Picket. There's more intelligence than what we shared in the meeting."

"There is?"

"It came just this morning. Captain Frye begged us not to share it. Wilfred and Helmer agreed with him."

"About our family?" Picket asked, an eager energy building within him.

"Yes."

"What is it?"

"We believe some of them are being held in the Shade Hills. Another blackstone deposit. Probably another mine. They bring in the strongest, freshest bucks to mine it dry, often accompanied by their sons. We think your father

65

and brother are there. It's near the route on which I travel to Kingston."

"Really? That's wonderful—"

Smalls held up a hand. "All my counselors say we shouldn't risk it and that you and the Fowlers will better serve the cause by training here."

"But if it isn't far, we could go and be back. Smalls—Your Highness, please!"

"They all say it's the wrong use of our limited forces."

"They've been saying that for months! But do they have family there?" Picket all but shouted. "Do they care?"

"Wilfred's brother is there," Smalls said. "He cares. We all care."

Picket spun and clenched at his ears in agitation. "They are so close? And you will do nothing? Heather would…"

"Heather would what?" Smalls asked, his face strained.

He almost didn't say it. He almost held it in. But he couldn't stop himself. "She would be ashamed to learn you didn't do it. If you could and didn't, it would be…it would be a betrayal."

"Betrayal?" Smalls leaned back and put his hands over his face. "I want to, Picket. All my heart is in it, but I cannot be impulsive. I must listen to wise counsel."

"It would mean everything to her," Picket said. "It would mean the world."

Smalls stood and paced. When he turned to face his friend, Picket could see the exhaustion in his eyes. "I will do what I can, my friend. For you, who saved me at the hallowed ground of my father's death. For your dear sister. I will do what I can."

"Thank you, Your Highness," Picket said, falling to one knee. "I wish I could be there with you."

"You cannot," he said. "I need you to stay here and protect my sister, and all those we love."

Picket nodded. "I will, my lord. I will do anything for you."

Smalls pulled Picket up and looked him in the eyes. "Good. Because there's something I need you to do for me. Give me your sword."

* * *

Not long after, Picket found Heather on the Fowlers' course. She sat, hugging her knees, head hanging down. He had determined to say nothing to her, or anyone else, of what Smalls had said and done. He sat beside her on the ground as the first star appeared through the tangled branches of a tree.

"A star in the tree," he said, pointing. She looked up. Then both of them lay down on their backs, staring at the star.

"We're too old to chase stars now," she said.

They lay there a few minutes in silence, watching the darkening sky.

"Are you avoiding Emma?" he asked.

"What can I do?" she said. "We tell each other

everything. I feel like I'm going to betray someone I love one way or the other."

"I know it's hard," he said. "But it's also simple. You cannot tell Emma who she is."

She was quiet for a long time. They watched as the sky slowly became a blackened canvas upon which appeared a thousand painted stars. "It was easy when we were only seeking one star," she said. "But now our sky is full of choices."

"I will always choose you, Heather," he said.

"And I, you," she agreed. "But what about Smalls and Emma? How can I choose between them?"

"We can never choose between Smalls and anyone else. The moment we do, the door is open to the kind of treachery our uncle chose."

"I will never betray Smalls," she said. "I only want to avoid betraying Emma—Princess Emma—too."

"I understand," Picket said. "Is there something else bothering you? Is it just that Smalls is leaving?"

She was silent again for a long while, and he let her be.

At last she spoke. "It's not only that he's leaving," she said, closing her eyes on tears.

Picket felt absently for his sword hilt, a chill spreading over him.

Chapter Eleven

A WHITE WOLF

Morbin's lair hummed with activity. Sween went about her duties while lords and generals arrived in large numbers. It was supposed to be an important day. The master slave of Morbin's house, an old red rabbit named Gritch, had warned them all to work quickly and to keep their heads down. Melody, a new slave much younger than Sween, had objected. But Gritch had made it clear that today they must be perfect. And silent. Sween was anxious, but she worked on as usual, trying to stay out of the way.

In the antechamber, a white wolf brushed past her, growling as he went. She jumped aside, lowering her gaze. He was tall and strong and wore a black vest over a charcoal tunic. The crest over his chest showed a black shield with a red diamond bent into a fang in its center.

A stout wolf beside him spoke. "I see that lunch has already arrived, General Flox." His laugh was a guttural rasp. She shivered and turned aside. What was to stop them from tearing her apart? Would Morbin object? No, he would only get a new slave to scrub his floors.

General Flox's face was set in a sneering snarl. "I believe Lord Morbin has prepared more tender meat for our meal today," he said. "I don't want to keep him waiting. We will have plenty of rabbits to devour soon enough."

"For the old captain's sake," the other wolf muttered, "I hope it's thousands."

"It might well be," Flox said, "if rumors prove true."

They moved on a few steps, leaving Sween shaken, her heart pounding in her chest as she bent over her work. She hoped they would move on, but they stopped in the doorway.

"Now that we're here, I'm uneasy," the stout wolf whispered. "Will Lord Morbin look at Garlackson's failure as a reason to break the pact, and the pack?"

"Be easy, Blenk. I told you. He needs us on the ground," Flox answered, his pale fur a bright blur in Sween's peripheral vision. "If we can hold our force under control and prevent any wildlings from gathering a following, Morbin will use us. We just have to assure him that we have our own in hand and that the old agreement still stands."

Sween's keen ears heard all, though she scrubbed on as if she were deaf. *Garlackson's failure?* She had heard other rumors over the past few months. There was a tense day at Morbin's court when an old familiar voice had reported woeful news to the enraged master hawk. She had heard that it was about the red-eyed wolf captain, but she knew no details for certain. In the rabbit camp, rumors flew, rumors of a brave flying rabbit who had killed the son of

King Garlacks and rescued Jupiter's heir. It sounded fanciful, the kind of story a slave would like to believe, a story to fuel hope. She wasn't sure what was true, but her heart burned when she heard of any setback for these Lords of Prey and their terrible allies.

She realized she had been daydreaming again, lost in a reverie of hopeful visions. A flying rabbit. A rescued prince. A check on the aggression of their oppressors. She had almost sung.

Again she silenced the song within her. But the silence, she noticed, was not only within her. The corridor was quiet. She glanced up at the two wolves. They had stopped talking. They were staring at her with squinting eyes and the beginnings of awful snarls.

She hadn't said anything, had she? Hadn't sung, surely. Gazing up at the pair, she waited in panicked silence for them to speak.

The white wolf strode forward, hand on the hilt of his sword. "What were you smiling at?"

She looked down. Had she smiled? Had she really been so foolish?

"Slaves must not smile," she said, almost in a whisper.

"No," General Flox said, tugging on his sword hilt, "they must *not*!"

Sween braced for the worst, but a call rang out from the corridor. "General Flox! Lord Morbin is seeking you! There's news of the attack."

Flox spun, sheathing his sword in a huff. He hurried

back down the hall and disappeared through the doorway with his companion.

Sween sagged, her breath returning in great heaving gasps. She was shaking again, shivering on the floor again. Terrified again.

I must never smile.

I must never sing.

Chapter Twelve

DUTY AND FRIENDSHIP

Picket woke early from a dreamless sleep. He sat up in his bunk and came more fully awake. Steady dread grew in him. He felt wary and keen, but for what, he didn't quite know. There was the sacred charge the prince had given him, Heather's fears about the prince, and the imminent threat against Halfwind Citadel. Not to mention that his family were still captives, or worse.

He looked around the bunkhouse; everyone he saw was still sleeping. There were lots of empty bunks. But most of those absent weren't simply out and about early; they were gone. That explained the wariness he felt. The absence of the prince, their uncle, and Lord Blackstar—all headed for Kingston, along with some of the best of their fighters—made him feel like he must be extra sharp. Lord Rake had also departed for Cloud Mountain, along with Pacer and those from the Forest Guard who made such a deadly force. All that remained was the usual complement of soldiers from this solitary citadel, led by Lord Ramnor and seconded by Captain Frye. Lord Ramnor was old, but

Captain Frye was even older and heavy and had only the use of one arm. He was still a deadly fighter, but Picket felt that much of the weight of defending the citadel now fell to the Fowlers. And, in a way, to himself.

He needed to find Master Helmer.

Picket leapt from his bed, landing quietly on the hard ground. He dressed quickly, then fastened his back-scabbard in place, rammed home his sword, and left the bunkhouse. As he wound through empty corridors, he reached out to touch the wooden slats that reinforced the dirt walls of the tunnels. He imagined the terror of being trapped in this old warren should it ever collapse. Halfwind was a winding warren of mixed material. Dirt walls gave way to stone arches; ruggedly practical accommodations lay not far from the ornate stonework of Leapers Hall.

He ran past the arched entrance to Leapers Hall and heard the early morning songs of the gathered votaries. Peeking inside as he jogged, he saw a blue blur of kneeling faithful. He had befriended some of the votaries, though it still seemed strange to him that these blue-robed rabbits lived alongside the soldiers and support staff that made up the center of this community. But the quiet votaries were usually kind, and many were devoted to a solitary pursuit for long years, only breaking their work for community meals and rituals. That was not unlike the life of a soldier. And some were soldiers, while others believed that fighting was unworthy of their order. Picket understood this belief, but for now he could see no other way. With the world as it was, he must be a soldier, and the best one he could possibly be. He moved on, the morning songs fading behind him.

Soon he was clear of the warren and out in the open air, jogging through a tunnel of the braided thorns that seemed to grow everywhere. He had lost count of how many of them Heather had plucked from his skin.

Heather.

He thought about trying to find her. He had walked her to her room the night before. She had said she hoped Emma was already asleep so she wouldn't have to talk to her. He hoped Heather was still resting, that she found solace in her sleep. He hoped she had come to accept that she must keep this secret from Emma—from the princess— for everyone's good. *Everyone, except a friend who probably deserves to know the truth*, he mused. So it still bothered him, this need for secrecy. There had been so much of it in the Longtreaders' own lives, he hated to be a part of concealing anything—especially something so important— from a dear friend. How could he keep such a thing from someone he cared for, from someone who had been like family to him and Heather when they were isolated, scared, and—himself especially—at their worst? Emma had stuck with him when bitterness and resentment had poisoned his life. He owed her so much. Didn't he owe her the truth? *This can't help. I know my duty.*

He went through the passage that approached the stationed sentinels. "A friend and fellow," he said, giving the passphrase.

"Pass on," came the reply. He did, jogging past the two tired rabbits, whose watch was nearly over. He heard them whisper as he disappeared around the corner. "That was him. The hero of Jupiter's Crossing…" They said more, but he could no longer hear. It was common for him to hear whispers, to be lauded by young soldiers. But he had no interest in the last fight, only the next one. This whispered awe from other rabbits only served to remind him of the expectations others had for him, of how much responsibility he carried for this vulnerable citadel suddenly bereft of its best.

He emerged onto the Fowlers' course, expecting it to be empty. But Perkinson was there, jogging back toward him.

"Good morning, Perk," Picket said.

"Morning, Pick," Perkinson replied. "I'm glad to see we're not all lazy." He was sweating, and he looked tired.

"Couldn't sleep?" Picket asked.

"Yeah. I was a little anxious since learning that half our fighting strength and most of our leadership skipped off in the night. No pressure on us, right?"

"Right," Picket said. "Sounds like you're well-informed. And now we have to protect—" He had almost said something about Emma, but he stopped himself.

"Protect…?"

Picket shrugged. "Did you hear about our new member?"

"The Blackstar kid? Cole?"

"Yeah."

"I've met him a few times," Perkinson said. "He seems okay. Doesn't talk much, but he's a fighter. I know that. They don't raise any other kind down at Kingston. Especially Lord Blackstar's son. They are a rare breed."

"Must be hard to live up to the expectation of a great family name," Picket said.

Perkinson was silent. He looked off into the trees. Evidently he didn't want to talk about his father, the legendary Perkin One-Eye, best friend of King Jupiter and hero of a hundred battles. "Sorry," Picket said. "It's none of my business. I'm sorry about your father."

"It's okay, Pick. I just want to make my own name. It's hard when it's right there every time anyone is talking to you."

"What do you want to be called?"

"Cuddles?" Perkinson said, jabbing Picket with a quick, friendly punch.

"Perfect," Picket said. "It suits you."

"Naw, I'll keep my name, and all the weight it brings with it. It keeps me sharp."

"So what brought you out so early?" Picket asked, motioning toward the course behind Perk. "Going through the paces?"

"Yeah," he said, laughing. "Speaking of staying sharp," he said, dancing in place and throwing a few more punches near Picket. "Always calms me down. What do you say?"

"I guess I came to do just that," Picket said. "But first I want some food."

"Let's get some," Perkinson said. Picket nodded, and the friends jogged toward the mess hall.

Picket liked Perkinson. He was energetic and upbeat and came from a storied family. Picket had been in awe of Perkinson when he arrived at Halfwind, but Perk had quickly put Picket at ease, and they fell into a fast friendship and became a potent attacking combo. Unlike Heyward, Perkinson was always reliable in their simulated attacks. He was quick, intelligent, and agile; he had it all when it came to being a soldier. And he should. He had been trained by the best from a very young age.

Even though Perkinson had already been at the course for who knew how long, Picket was laboring to keep up with him.

"You need to warm up," Perkinson said over his shoulder.

"We'll see about that!" Picket said, picking up his pace and surging ahead. Perkinson in turn sped up and overtook Picket. Soon the two young rabbits were hurtling through the narrow tunnels, racing to the mess hall, making more noise than anyone should at such an early hour.

Rounding a dark corner, neck and neck, Picket felt something catch his foot. He pitched forward, knocking into Perk. Both rabbits smashed into the wall and broke through a collection of wooden slats with a loud crack. Picket rolled and crashed to a halt. Perkinson slid beside him. Earth gave way, spilling a heap of dirt onto their heads.

Opening his eyes, Picket saw a blade before him in the

dim hallway. He followed the blade upward to its handle and saw a green emerald sparkling in the hilt. Peering into the dark countenance above, he recognized Captain Helmer.

"You two idiots get the rest up and out on the course in ten minutes," Helmer said gruffly, sheathing his sword. "Instead of acting like two younglings, why don't you show some responsibility? This isn't a game of Bouncer we're playing, lads. We just lost most of the experience and leadership in Halfwind. And don't forget, there's an army closing in!"

"Yes, Captain," the bucks said together, knocking dirt from their heads and scrambling to their feet. Perkinson went on, "We were just going to the mess."

"You *are* a mess," Helmer said, glaring at their dirty, sweaty fur. "Both of you."

"We're sorry, Master," Picket said. "We'll get the other Fowlers. Should we invite Coleden Blackstar?"

"Of course," Helmer said, turning. "He's one of us now." The old black rabbit stormed off.

Picket gently elbowed Perk. "Why do you always seem to get me in trouble?"

"Because neither of us likes to lose," Perk said, adding some more dirt to Picket's head.

"I'm just glad that in the big fight," Picket said, shaking the dirt off his head, "we're both on the same side."

Perkinson stood and placed his hand over his heart. "Till the Green Ember rises, or the end of the world."

Picket returned the salute. Then they hurried toward the bunkhouse.

Chapter Thirteen

A Red Sunrise

Heather left her bed before Emma was awake. She went to the library, which was attached to Lord Ramnor's ready room. Lord Ramnor sat beside the fire, reading.

"Am I disturbing you?" she whispered.

"Of course not, Heather," he said, removing his glasses and beckoning her over. "It's cold and grey out there. A bad omen."

"Do you read omens, Lord Ramnor, or read of omens?" she asked, nodding at his book. He reminded her of Father. Though Lord Ramnor was much older, his bearing was as much a scholar's as that of a military commander. She saw how it all weighed on him and admired him for his perseverance. He fought because of what he loved, not because he loved to fight.

"I'm reading children's poems," he said, "to clear my mind before the day's tasks. I have done it for years—whenever I can."

"Children's poetry, a great lord like you?" she asked. "Does it distract you?"

"No," he answered. "Well, I suppose it does. But I feel less—I don't know—less sullied by the awful parts of my work when I read." She nodded and he went on, returning his glasses to his nose. "Consider this one, Heather. One even the Scribe of the Cause would be proud of." She smirked but listened as he began.

> *"'Who was it stole the apple pie?'*
> *"Twasn't I, 'Twasn't I'*
> *'Who stole, then?' rings her reply,*
> *still I deny, still I deny.*
> *Asked I am why I should lie,*
> *'I am innocent,' I cry,*
> *but inside I know who stole the pie,*
> *for 'twas I, for 'twas I,*
> *'twas I who stole the apple pie*
> *but shall deny it till I die.*
> *Inside I know who stole the pie*
> *for there it lies, in my insides."*

Heather smiled wearily. "It's sweet, and funny. But so deceitful."

"Fitting for our times," he sighed, rising. Then, with a quick bow and a smile, he walked out.

Heather stood with her back to the fire, her appetite now whispering about apple pie. She glanced at the fire, touched her necklace charm and sighed, then crossed to Lord Ramnor's desk. She took up the book of poems and sat down. Maybe this could help expel her gloom. She sat for a while with the book, laughing here and there, until she sensed the dawn approaching.

She would be wanted on the Fowlers' course. How long could she avoid Emma? How long could she live with this lie inside her? She rose and crossed the room, hesitating by the door. She wanted to return to the chair by the fire and read all day.

But there is work to do. Like Lord Ramnor, she would do her duty. She inhaled deeply and walked through the door.

What she saw froze her blood.

* * *

Picket wanted to complain to Helmer. His master had yelled at him and Perk for running through the halls, then forced them to run even more through the halls in order to get everyone to the course in less than ten minutes. But Picket didn't dare say anything. Helmer didn't want to hear that right now, he was sure. *Good thing he can't read my thoughts.*

"Stay focused, Lieutenant," Helmer said sharply to Picket.

"Yessir!"

The Fowlers were lined up, backs to the trail and faces toward their captain. Helmer stood in front of the Fowlers' course and the forest beyond. They stood in a row: long-legged Jo Shanks, steady Perkinson, Picket, and their new member, Coleden Blackstar. Heather was not there yet.

"Bucks, this is Coleden, our new friend from the southeast," Helmer said, nodding at the tall black rabbit whose famous ancestor was King Whitson Mariner's savior. "We recruited him because we didn't already have enough cocky rabbits from famous, or infamous, families." He smirked. "Coleden is new. Raw. Inexperienced in our arts. He needs to learn, probably through great pain, what it means to be a Fowler."

Picket glanced at Coleden, saw the quiet confidence in his face. Perkinson looked tense, uneasy, while Jo was laughing behind his hand. But Picket felt sorry for the new recruit. No matter what kind of dangers he had faced at Kingston, no one could be ready for Helmer.

"You must be prepared to go head-to-head in the tree-tops with the most vicious creatures, the monsters of your ancestors' tales," Helmer went on. Picket watched Coleden's face. It went from focused attention to distraction. He seemed to be looking past Helmer. "You will run toward danger, not away," the old master went on, his voice getting louder and his eyes narrowing. "You will meet their best aloft. You will fly."

Picket grew concerned for Coleden. He was only half paying attention. Helmer had clearly noticed and was seething.

"Do we have a problem, son?" Helmer said, planting himself right in front of the young buck. Picket knew that

Helmer would strike soon and Coleden would end up on his back.

"We might," Coleden said, looking past Helmer. Then, before Helmer could speak again, Coleden dove at the captain, knocking him to the ground just as an arrow whizzed through the air above them. It had come from the forest, and more followed quickly after. Picket dove sideways and caught Jo, dragging him down just as a hail of arrows filled the sky. Perk had already moved, but Picket collided with Jo just as an arrow caught Jo's arm, spinning him down.

Perk was on his feet, rushing back to the tunnel. The remaining Fowlers found cover behind several wooden wolves fitted with blades.

Helmer rolled over and drew his sword. Jo and Coleden had theirs out at once. They all made as if to run, but Coleden held up a hand as arrows filled the sky.

"It's too late," he said.

"Can you reach your bow, Jo?" Helmer grunted as he peered out from the insufficient cover in an effort to see the enemy.

"No," Jo grunted.

"He's hurt," Picket said, reaching for Jo's arm, where an arrow was lodged.

"Pull it out," Helmer said, glancing at the wound before returning his attention to the trees. The wound wasn't deep, and Picket trusted Helmer's instincts. He looked at Jo, who nodded, and pulled the arrow out as Jo stifled a scream.

85

Tearing off a piece of cloth, Picket wrapped the wound as best he could. He turned to Helmer.

"What's the situation?"

"We're pinned," Helmer said.

"They're waiting on something. Surely it's not just that they need to account for us?" Coleden said, pointing to the tree line. Picket saw that it was alive with enemies.

"The tall rabbits?" Picket asked.

"I don't think so," Coleden said, "unless they have wolves with them." As he spoke, several wolves broke through the tree line and charged them. Covering arrows sped above them as they came. Coleden pulled Helmer to the ground as most of the deadly darts passed over their heads. Others thudded into their wooden protectors.

"We need a bow," Jo said.

"We need a rescue," Coleden said. Picket hated to admit it, but there it was. The elite Fowlers, on the grim occasion of their first real combat, needed rescuing. The wolves were nearly on them.

Picket drew his sword and positioned himself in front of Jo.

"I'm okay," Jo said. "There are too many for you to protect me."

There were.

Six wolves rushed toward the four trapped rabbits. They tore the ground with their pounding claws. Helmer took a last look over the flimsy barricade and called out, "Rush them!"

Leaping over the wooden wolf, Picket sped toward the attacking wolves. Now he could see their numbers. There were hundreds in the woods. The four rabbits charged in, each seeming unwilling to be the last to the clash. Arrows whizzed by, and Picket weaved back and forth, hoping to throw them off. There were precious few advantages for rabbits at war with wolves, but Picket planned to exploit them all for as long as he could. Rabbits were fast, could dodge and cut with tremendous speed. They had powerful feet, if given enough time to leap and strike. They were self-controlled and cunning, with their weapons and their strategy.

And the heirs of Flint and Fay were brave.

Picket coiled for a terrific leap. He launched high and flipped forward, landing a thundering kick on the foremost wolf. He felt the crack of impact, saw the wolf give way as he landed and rolled into a shorter jump to strike out with his blade. This met a shield and rattled his wrists. He held on and deflected the return strike from a jabbing spear. He dodged and struck, leapt back and surged forward, dimly aware of the desperate struggles all around him.

After half a minute of madness, he saw the wolves giving way, and he realized that more rabbits were among them. As Picket deftly blocked a sword thrust in front, a slavering wolf, teeth bared, surged for his shoulder. Out of nowhere, a rabbit kick met the wolf's jaws, knocking him sideways. Perkinson landed beside him, an attachment of Halfwind soldiers joining in. Perkinson finished the wolf with his blade and grabbed at Picket.

"Let's go, Longtreader," he said, looking wildly all around. "Back! Back!" he shouted. Picket saw Coleden flip backward and strike out at a wolf that had pinned Jo, then dart sideways to fend off another attacker as the surge of soldiers met the line. He looked calm, natural. He swung his sword like it was part of his strong arm.

"Fall back!" Picket shouted.

Helmer ended the wolf he had been locked in combat with, then staggered back, grabbing Jo. More and more wolves poured from the forest as the soldiers from the citadel flooded out to meet them, warriors in white tunics, a red moon crossed with spears on their chests. Among them ran a cluster of blue-robed rabbits, armed and fierce as they joined battle with the wolves.

Picket saw, before he fell into the temporary safety of the tunnel passage, that the wolves outnumbered the rabbits three to one.

It would be a slaughter.

Chapter Fourteen

Bear the Flame

W e have to get back out there!" Picket shouted.

"Hold, Lieutenant!" Helmer called, panting. Picket saw that his fur was wet with sweat and blood and his leg was badly injured.

"Heather," Picket said. Jo, Coleden, and Perkinson were all gasping for breath, eyes darting, looking forward out the tunnel and back toward the citadel. "We need a medic. I'll get her."

"Hold!" Helmer shouted again. "Remember your wits, bucks. What's our duty?"

"Secure the lord," Perkinson said. "Defend the citadel. Beat back the advance."

"That's right. Picket," Helmer shouted. The din from outside was awful. "You and Perk get in there and secure vital personnel!"

"What about you?" Picket shouted.

"Obey your orders, bucks!"

Picket heard and obeyed. Leaving their three companions, two of whom were hurt, he and Perkinson raced toward the citadel. One backward glance showed Picket that Helmer was sending Jo inside, probably for treatment, while he and Coleden charged back into the fight.

Once inside, Perkinson turned right, rushing for Lord Ramnor's rooms. That's when Picket realized what his true duty was. "Go on!" he shouted. Perk had a wild look in his eyes but nodded quickly. He barreled through the corridor and was gone.

Picket charged back toward the hospital. Toward Emma, daughter of King Jupiter the Great, whose life he had sworn to protect.

* * *

Heather couldn't believe what she was seeing. A wolf! *Inside* Halfwind Citadel. She was shocked, but her shock quickly gave way to anger. She sped back into the room and seized a large burning brand from the fire. Gripping the unlit end, she rushed back into the hall, a wild anger driving her on.

The wolf was gone.

The tunnel began to fill with screams, with the sounds of scattering rabbits, with the half-disciplined scurrying of a citadel under siege. She had seen this once before, at Cloud Mountain. But that had been a trap, a ruse. This might be a full-scale attack.

Terror rose within her, but she fought it down. She scolded a few whimpering rabbits nearby, reminding them to do their duty. They nodded and ran on. Then she remembered that she herself had a duty. She ran toward the hospital, still carrying the flaming brand. She bore it like a torch and raced through the dirt-packed walls of the warren, stopping for nothing.

Rabbits gave way before her, and she shouted encouragement to everyone she passed. "Fight! For the Mended Wood and Jupiter's heir!"

* * *

Picket reached the hospital and quickly joined in the fight, taking on a wolf near the main door. With some help from another soldier, he soon had the better of the invader and drove him out, wounded. Picket surveyed the large room. The stone pillars and artful arches held up the ceiling of a wide room, usually tidy and serene. But all was chaos now. Patients huddled in a corner while a few soldiers tried to contend with several wolves. He scanned for Emma and spotted her. She was standing in front of a frightened group of sick younglings, her arms spread out in front of them. It would do little good.

Three wolves came for them, loping past the side door and trapping her and her patients in a corner. Heyna Blackstar lay on the floor nearby. She wasn't moving.

Picket was attacked again. He did his best to break free, but this wolf was a terrific scrapper, and Picket had to fight hard just to stay alive. He swung his sword at the wolf, but his stroke was blocked. The wolf lashed out with his powerful claws and knocked Picket back, bloodied and dazed.

Picket rolled over and stole a glance at the side door as the wolf closed in on him. He saw Emma, magnificent in her defiance. She was every ounce a princess then. No one could doubt it if they looked at her now. She didn't budge an inch as the three wolves attacked. Then Jo was beside him, and together they drove back the wolf. Picket turned and charged for the far corner. He knew he would be too late.

Then he saw her.

Through the side door came Heather, with fury in her face and a fiery brand in her hands. She lunged for the three wolves, smashing the burning brand into the nearest. It broke over his head, and as he fell an explosion of sparks and flaming splinters spread over the next wolf.

That slowed them down, at least for a moment. The first, howling in rage as his singed fur sizzled, turned on Heather and sprang at her. But Picket was there, deflecting his deadly stroke and silencing him with his own flashing blade. Jo met the second with the same result, and Emma was faced with only one attacker. She didn't flinch, only stayed in front of the younglings, whispering assurances to them as the wolf sprang.

Picket leapt and met him in midair, a rending crack sounding as they spun and fell, sprawling on the ground. Jo led an eager band to secure the wolf.

Heather was by Emma's side. "Are you okay?" she asked. Picket sprang to his feet and joined her.

"Are you all right, Emma?"

"I'm fine!" Emma said, shaking her head and checking the younglings. "Thanks, you two."

Heather and Picket stood dumbly beside Emma. She frowned. "We all have work here. Let's get to it."

Picket realized that she was telling him to leave her alone and do his duty. *She doesn't know who she is or how important her life is. She would give it away in a moment if it meant saving someone else.*

Emma stared at Picket and Heather for a moment, then pushed past them to Heyna, bending to tend the fallen doe.

Heather and Picket put their heads together.

"What do we do now?" he asked.

"I don't know," she said. "We have to protect her, first of all."

Captain Frye came in, eyes darting back and forth, a gang of soldiers with him. When he saw Emma, he sighed with relief, then ordered his soldiers to secure the room. Picket ran to him.

"What now, Captain?"

"She's safe," he said, wheezing terribly. "I can't find Lord Ramnor, and the battle is all but lost. It's awful out there."

"What should we do?" Picket asked.

"Emma's okay, but stay close to her, Heather," he whispered. "Try to find Lord Ramnor and then get the princess out of here."

"And me?"

"Back to the battle!" he shouted, and he ran off.

Picket hugged Heather, then handed her his sword. "To protect yourself," he said. "And Heather, protect it, too."

Heather nodded and ran off down the warren's winding tunnels. Picket bent and grabbed a sword left by a fallen fellow soldier. As he turned to follow Captain Frye, his eyes met Emma's. She smiled at him, a weary, wonderful smile. He felt in that moment that he would gladly lay down his life for her.

And perhaps he would. Perhaps this day.

He caught up to Captain Frye as they reached the outside tunnel, and they followed it until it issued into daylight. Horrible sounds filled the air. Picket broke through the tunnel wall, Captain Frye behind him. They scanned the field. A cold breeze was blowing, and the sky was grey. The rabbit line was crumbling. The wolves advanced. A last huddle of rabbits held the ground surrounding the tunnel gate. Picket and Captain Frye rushed to join them. Picket knew it was hopeless.

"To the end of the world!" Captain Frye shouted.

Picket believed it was.

Chapter Fifteen

AN END AND A BEGINNING

Heather dashed toward Lord Ramnor's rooms, hoping that he might have returned. There were wounded rabbits everywhere, and she didn't know what to do. She ran on, aiming for the least awful thing. Her life was dedicated to healing. She didn't like the feel of the sword in her hands, but she would do what she had to do.

At last she drew near the ready room and, hearing an agonized cry from within, rounded the final curve and bolted inside. She saw Perkinson, kneeling over the fallen form of Lord Ramnor. A scream escaped her mouth, and she dropped Picket's sword. The blade clattered on the stone. Perkinson turned, a panicked expression on his face. He blinked, stammered for a moment, and then shouted, "Heather! Help him!"

Heather knelt by the wounded lord. At a glance, she could tell it was bad. A wound bloomed on his chest, and Heather knew at once he would never rise again. She turned to see Perkinson pacing, a pained expression on his face.

Lord Ramnor coughed, then tried to speak. Perkinson rushed over.

"What is it, lord?" Heather said.

"There it…" Lord Ramnor wheezed, "lies…" He seemed to be trying to move his hand, but he lacked the strength. He could only stare at his useless fingers.

"The poem?" Heather whispered, tears burning her eyes. "The poem from this morning?" she asked.

But he was gone. She bowed her head.

"Is he—?" Perkinson asked.

"Yes," she whispered. Silence followed. How long, Heather couldn't tell.

Finally Perkinson spoke again. "A mighty lord has fallen," he said. "Now who will lead us?"

* * *

Picket leaned into the battle with all his remaining strength. However many moments were left to him, he would spend them here on this field fighting for the cause he loved, for those he loved. He found Helmer, rushed to fight beside him, and sent his sword flying at the enemy. He saw Helmer's Fowlers' patch, that emblem of a flying rabbit, and the sight saddened him. All of their preparations, their gallant plans to take the war to their enemies on the heights. For what? He would die in a muddled mass of soldiers crowded on the ground.

The clamor of battle resounded through the field, and

he was vaguely aware that they were being driven back on all sides, that the rabbits were all but beaten. Despair flooded his heart.

Snow began to fall, light flakes drifting down in slow, swaying arcs.

Then came a tremendous shout and a rumbling of horns. Picket tried to think through the battle fog. What could make such a sound? It resonated in his heart like hope.

Then he saw them—an army of black-clad rabbits, armed with flashing lances and wearing silver breastplates. They were hurrying toward the battle. In the fore ran a large rabbit, gleaming in silver armor, a silver crown upon his head. Above him flew a black star-filled banner.

Picket's tired mind didn't know what to make of it, but he remembered the scouts' report. He wondered if this was the last devastating piece of the puzzle, the attack that would finish all of Halfwind. But—no. The tall rabbits moved toward the wolves with force, not beside them as allies. With speed and fury, they attacked them as enemies.

Picket leapt for joy.

The new rabbit army fell on the wolves like a crushing wave, driving into them, and through them, with such force that Picket and his comrades felt an immediate relief in their own brutal contests. The wolves were turning, falling back. Helmer's eyes widened, and Picket, exhausted and light-headed, began to laugh. They sagged, gulped precious air, then joined in the last incredible push against the wolf army.

It happened fast. Picket searched for the Silver Prince, saw him blazing away in the thickest part of the battle. A special guard of rabbits surrounded him, all armored in black with silver stars on their shields. They were the deadliest fighters Picket had ever seen. Together they formed an impenetrable pocket around their prince, and while his flanks were so well protected, he fought with wild confidence.

Picket gaped in wonder. Who was this rabbit who fought like a god beneath a banner of stars? Was it King Jupiter back from the grave? Who else could fight like this? Who else could command so deadly a force?

Then he saw that all the Halfwind rabbits watched in awe, resting on their swords as the Silver Prince and his black attackers drove the wolf army back in a terrific advance. The Halfwind rabbits cheered, and Picket joined in, as the last wolves were forced into a corner.

"Who could they be?" Picket called out to Helmer.

"I don't know," Helmer wheezed. "But they have certainly saved us all. It reminds me of long ago."

"In King Jupiter's day?" Picket asked.

"No," Helmer said, "from before."

Picket frowned. *What can he mean?* Picket was about to ask when he remembered Emma, Heather, and Lord Ramnor. "Emma!" he said, and he dashed back toward the tunnel. Helmer followed him in, limping as he went.

They passed by the gate, now wrecked, and charged through tunnel after tunnel until they came to the hospital. Picket ran inside and saw that more wolves had entered.

Once again, Emma and the younglings were threatened. Picket saw Heather beside her, sword in hand. While Emma kept her vigilant guard, five massive rabbits in black armor dispatched the last of the wolves. Actually, Picket noticed, they weren't all so large. The middle rabbit was not much bigger than himself, but like the fierce captain out in the battle whom Picket thought of as the Silver Prince, this shorter rabbit also wore a silver crown. A small crown made of silver stars. With two warriors on his right and two on his left, this second Silver Prince delivered the final blow to the defeated wolves and turned, breathing hard, to Emma. He seemed to be checking on her safety. She was unharmed, though her face was frozen in alarm and confusion.

Now Picket saw the rabbit who had saved her. He saw a familiar face. He saw the gold-and-silver fur, so like his own. He couldn't believe his eyes.

"Kyle?" Emma said, dumbfounded.

One of his black-clad companions bowed, took off his helmet, and spoke. "This is Prince Kylen, son of King Bleston, Second Lord of Terralain, and the heir of all Natalia."

Kyle smiled, that old winning smile, with only the faintest hint of embarrassment. He looked at Emma and the Longtreaders. "I'm glad to see you, old friends."

Chapter Sixteen

A NEW ORDER

For three days and two nights the after-battle work occupied Heather's every waking moment. There was so much to do—care for the wounded, bury the dead, adjust their routine to the new order that arrived with their surprising victory.

Heather and Picket walked the halls, headed for an audience with Prince Bleston, the long-absent brother of King Jupiter the Great. The citadel was calling him the Silver Prince. They now knew that for years he had been ruler of the hidden city of Terralain, a place once believed to be legendary. But Terralain had been real after all. *At least Kyle didn't lie about that.*

Heather was tired, and her heart was full of confused emotions. She was so happy the citadel had been saved, so grateful that those she loved most had been preserved. But she was brokenhearted about Lord Ramnor, terribly sad that she had been there at the end but could not save him. Perhaps Doctor Zeiger or Emma could have saved him, but not her. He had been her particular friend, was like family to her. She couldn't even figure out what his last words meant. "There it…lies." There *what* lies? It bothered her.

Still worse was Kyle. Or Prince Kylen, as he was now called. He had betrayed Smalls to Morbin and had invited an attack on Cloud Mountain. Many good rabbits had lost their lives. Yet he walked through the halls of Halfwind Citadel as an honored hero. And hero he was, she had to admit. He had saved Emma, herself, and many others. His army had won a tremendous victory, rescuing Halfwind from certain doom. But beyond the betrayal of the cause and the community at Cloud Mountain, Kyle had lied to *her*. He had been *her* friend, and he betrayed *her*. She was ashamed that this was what angered her most.

"How are we supposed to go in there and say thank you to Kyle?" Picket asked. "I can't do that."

"Captain Frye believes it best if we just go along with things for now," she answered, "until Smalls and the other lords get back."

"Is Captain Frye even in charge?"

"He is to me," she said. "But it's a good question, Pick. Prince Bleston has occupied Lord Ramnor's ready room. He calls for audiences, and we come when we're called. So you tell me."

"Seems like he's in charge."

"And his son," she said, smirking.

"I can't believe Kyle is really a prince, that he really came from Terralain. He's Smalls' cousin!"

"I don't know what to believe." She sighed and rubbed her eyes. "I'm glad we're alive, but I want to sleep for a week and wake up when the world makes sense."

"Since Lord Ramnor is dead, doesn't that mean Captain Frye should lead?" Picket asked.

"Yes. Emma says that the senior captain is supposed to take temporary command until the lords in council appoint someone to replace the fallen lord."

"The truth is," Picket said, lowering his voice as he looked around, "Emma has some claim to lead here."

"If she only knew who she was," Heather said, rubbing her head again. She felt so tired and confused. She just wanted this audience to be over so she could sleep.

They walked on, winding through the halls now occupied by a mix of Halfwind rabbits, votaries, and soldiers and the large newcomers from Terralain. The new rabbits were clad in black and wore bright silver breastplates.

"These Terralain rabbits are tough," Picket whispered. "They almost never talk, but you can see how strong they are. They move with power and purpose. You can't imagine how they fought, Heather. It was amazing. Especially Bleston. He was unbeatable, even against wolves."

"I seem to hear nothing but praise from everyone about him."

Picket smiled. "It was astonishing. You know how we used to dream of seeing King Jupiter in his glory? Well, I think now I know what it must have been like. I mean, Bleston is the old king's older brother, and if Jupiter was anything like Bleston, then I understand why everyone was in awe of him."

"But Bleston hated Jupiter," Heather said, her brows knitting. "I mean, Bleston left, right? That's what Uncle Wilfred said. He said that when their father, King Walter, passed over Bleston to give the Green Ember to Jupiter—to make him his heir—Bleston nearly started a war. He didn't, in the end. He left with a company of malcontents."

"And now he's back," Picket said. "And King Jupiter is gone."

"But Smalls isn't," Heather said with a sigh. "Oh, I wish Smalls were here."

"What if," Picket asked, "Heather, what if what we were told about Bleston was just King Jupiter's side of the story? What if Bleston's side tells it differently?"

They were getting closer. Picket slowed, and Heather matched his pace. "I don't know what to think, Pick. I'm tired."

"You've been working hard," he said, putting his arm around her. "Whatever happens, you and I are sticking together."

"Of course."

Heather looked up and saw Heyward passing by. She was surprised to see him dressed in a blue robe. He carried a rod in each hand, and he was touching them together at ends that were fitted with some kind of black metal fasteners. He connected, then disconnected them, frowning at how they locked together. "Heyward!" she said, grabbing his arm.

"Heather," he said. A smile appeared, replacing the concentrated frown he had worn. "And Picket. My friends! I had been reliably informed that you both survived, and I'm ever so glad to see it's true."

"And you. Are you well?" Picket asked. "I haven't seen you in the bunkhouse. Have you joined the order?"

"I am very well," he said. "And yes, I have joined."

"Is it good for you?" Heather asked.

"Yes. I believe it is," he said. Heather nodded, inviting him to go on. "You see, Heather, I was in the battle, thinking, as we all did, that I was about to die. And I realized that I had never finished anything of value in my life. I realized my work at Cloud Mountain was good, but not special, and that I had failed as a soldier and was about to die as one. I was simply brimming with regret."

"I understand that," Picket said.

"Beside me, I saw one of the blue-robed votaries. He was fighting desperately, just like the rest. But he was different. He looked assured, even in the face of certain death. And then I saw the Silver Prince and what he did. I was in awe, and a feeling of incredible gratitude came over me. I thought, if I was ever in that place of certain death again, that I wanted to be glad of what I'd done in my life. So, after the battle, I went to the brothers. I am an initiate now."

"Are you happy?" Heather asked, placing her hand tenderly on his shoulder.

"Yes," he said, patting her hand. "I can focus on a task, interrupted only by the most gratifying rites. I believe I will be at home among the brothers. And I have joined the activist branch, so I will still fight when the need is great. I haven't abandoned the cause. The votaries are loyalists, all." He smiled. "I am working on a project," he said, raising the two rods. "Most likely it won't work, but I shall give it my very best."

"Dear Heyward," Heather said. "We have an audience with Prince Bleston, so we must go. But we are so glad to see you well."

"And I, you, friends," Heyward said, touching his eyes, ears, and mouth in turn. "May your feet find the next stone."

They nodded, smiling, and walked on, coming to the door of what had been Lord Ramnor's rooms. Five stout rabbits guarded the door. They were dressed as all the other Terralain soldiers, but with one subtle variation. These rabbits wore red capes, and their polished shoulder armor bore the sign of Terralain, silver stars on a black field. Two stood at rigid attention on either side of the door, pikes and shields at the ready. One stood blocking the open door. Heather peeked past him and saw glimpses of the way Bleston had changed Lord Ramnor's rooms. There were new, elaborate tapestries, a table piled with food, more guards at the ready. Bleston was decked out in silver and seated in a massive chair on a platform near the fire.

"We're here to see the Silver Prince," Heather said, trying to push past the burley guard. He moved to block her, causing her to bump him. She tripped backward, and Picket caught her.

"What's that for? We were summoned," Picket said, moving in front of Heather. His hands rose, clenching into fists.

"That's not necessary, Picket." The voice was familiar. From behind the immovable guard, Kyle appeared. Heather's insides churned. Here he was, this handsome, charming, disarming scoundrel. He smiled kindly, his eyes showing that same hint of sadness they had held when he had been recognized after the battle. "Let them in," he said to the guard. The guard gave way at once, bowing. Kyle motioned for them to enter.

As they entered, Heather saw Picket's elbow find the big guard, and she looked away. Anger was brewing in her brother—and in her. She worried he would do something foolish.

Kyle stopped them once they were inside. At the far end of the room, Prince Bleston was speaking in low tones to several rabbits who were gathered around him.

"I consider the past as gone," Kyle said, "and we do well to forget it. We must be friends again."

"What's in the past, Kyle, and what we can't forget, Princeling," Heather said, "is our friendship destroyed, our friends murdered, and our future king betrayed."

Kyle looked down. "I'm not Kyle now—not the prankster you knew. I'm a prince, an heir, a warrior. I'm Kylen. I've done many things I'm not proud of, but all for the greater good."

"So you can rule the world?" Picket said.

"So that everyone can be free and equal," Kyle said. He seemed to believe what he said. But he had always been a convincing liar. Heather wanted to spit.

She looked around the room, at the splendid banners, the elaborate lamps, the indulgent table. "It looks like you're a little above equal. I'd like to see some of this food down at the hospital where we're trying to recover from this attack."

"At the hospital where we saved you? That hospital?" Kyle said, an edge in his voice. "Trying to recover from the attack where *our* army—" He stopped, took a deep breath, and continued in a civil whisper. "I understand your anger. I do. But as your friend—and I still count you as friends—I urge you to listen to Father. Please."

As if on cue, Bleston finished his conference and dismissed his attendants. He waved them over. "Prince Kylen," he called. "Bring your friends to me."

They went, and Heather saw Bleston for the first time. He was grey-furred and large, dressed in silver with light armor across his chest. He wore a crown of silver stars, a little larger and a lot taller than Kyle's. And he wore it well. The first soldiers who saw his charge in the battle had, like Picket, called him the Silver Prince, and the name had stuck.

He sat on a raised platform, with several other chairs placed in an arc. His was the largest chair, and the rest were unoccupied. He looked magnificent, regal, and imposing. So Heather was surprised to see the kindness in his eyes. He was smiling broadly.

As they approached, she understood what Picket meant about feeling the awe that one must have felt in the presence of King Jupiter. Here was one of royal blood, a descendant of King Whitson and so many mighty sires. Though moments before her mind was filled with things she meant to say, objections she meant to make, now she was silent, still, and deferential. She glanced at Picket, who seemed likewise undone. They were, to be sure, in the presence of greatness.

She felt a strong urge to bow. She resisted, but only barely.

"Greetings to you, Longtreaders," he said, and his voice rumbled with a happy authority. "I have heard of your prowess, and I think you shall make an excellent king and queen in Natalia."

Chapter Seventeen

THE WINTER KING

King and queen? Picket was puzzled, but he stood there, resisting the urge to bow, unable to think of anything to say.

"You are surprised I think of you as royalty?" Bleston laughed.

"Because we are not," Heather said, finding her tongue at last. Picket was grateful, because for him, the words wouldn't come.

"But you have behaved like royalty," he said. "Distinguishing yourselves. Showing you deserve to be free. In Terralain, all rabbits are free, and all are equal. All kings and queens—if only they will grab it."

"All equal?" Picket stammered. "But you are—"

"In Terralain," Bleston said, "we are all stars in the same night." He pointed to the banner, a black field filled with silver stars.

"Then why do all these serve you?" Heather asked, motioning to the attentive rabbits of Bleston's court.

"Well, I am a bit more than a king. I am the king who

makes all kings. I am king and kingmaker. I am effect and cause," he said, laughing.

"But can they oppose you?" Picket said, finally able to form a sentence.

"Of course they can," he said, winking at Kyle, "if they believe they are able." He laughed again, and Kyle smiled.

"So how is Terralain different than any other kingdom?"

"It is a kingdom for all kingdoms. It is a kingdom with a mission to make all kingdoms free and equal—all stars in the same night."

"But you are the sun in this sky," Heather asked, "are you not?"

He smiled again, then laughed loudly. "I like you, Heather Longtreader," he said. Then, looking at Kyle, he added, "You were right about her."

Kyle smiled, but Picket thought he looked the slightest bit uncomfortable. He had his father's easy way, his strong confidence and cheerful bravado. But was it only a mask?

"If you are, and possibly everyone else is, a king," Picket asked, "then does it bother you when they call you the Silver Prince?" Picket was trying to keep a wall around his heart, a wall made partly of anger toward Kyle for the betrayal in which his father had no doubt played a part. But he found he had to keep building it up again and again. Bleston's presence was powerful. Picket felt himself drawn to this strong, profoundly confident rabbit. *He's just the sort of leader we need*, he thought, before shaking his head to clear it.

"No," Bleston said, laughing. He looked past them toward the door, and Picket followed his gaze. There were more rabbits waiting to see him. One was Captain Frye. "I don't mind the name. It's quite poetic."

"But you are a prince," Heather said.

"Every king is a prince as well. I am a king, like my father and his father, all the way back to Whitson Mariner himself." As he said this, Bleston pulled at the chain of gold that hung around his neck, removing it from beneath his shirt and armor. Dangling from the chain was a bright red diamond. "I carry the Whitson Stone, and I am, by rights, the ruler of all Natalia."

Heather gasped. *The Whitson Stone?* She didn't know all the history, but she did know that, just as the emerald gem known as the Green Ember was the sign that the owner was to inherit the throne *someday*, the Whitson Stone meant the bearer was the rightful ruler *now*. She hadn't known where the stone was. She just assumed that Smalls or Lord Rake had it. Had King Jupiter lost it during his rule, or had it been stolen by Bleston after Jupiter's fall? Had the fallen king reigned without ever having it? Why hadn't Uncle Wilfred and Lord Rake mentioned it?

She found her voice again. "We have a king, or will soon, the true heir to your brave brother, who bore the Green Ember and ruled so well. His son and heir is destined for the throne. He will make us free, not call us kings and make us grovel. He will let us be who we are, inspire us to be who we ought, not promise us what we can never be."

"You don't believe you will be a queen?" he asked, his eyes keen and penetrating.

This went to her heart. The truth was, she did hope to be queen. Not because of a desire for power or prestige, but because she loved Smalls, and that was the only way to stay by his side for life. She bowed her head.

Bleston smiled a knowing, mischievous smile. "How about this, my friends?" he said, his tone calm and reassuring. "I will be for you a winter king, and we shall see if your small king shall ever return. If he does, we will talk about the new world together." He made a subtle signal, and Kyle motioned to the Longtreaders to move toward the door. "Thank you, young ones, for visiting me. We will talk further another time. Until then, carry on with your duties."

Their conference was over, ended with an order. There was no doubt who commanded in this place. *Was that the purpose of the meeting?* They saw Captain Frye just ahead. He was being led to Bleston by an unbelievably large rabbit with unique markings on his left shoulder armor, a splash of red Picket couldn't quite make out.

Picket moved close to Captain Frye and stood in front of him and his giant escort. "Lord Captain," Picket said, bowing his head. "Heather and I will continue in our duty but await any further orders from you." He finished in a salute. The giant guard glowered at him. Captain Frye smiled tightly and pulled Picket close.

"Be careful, son," he whispered close to Picket's ear. "These aren't the kind to play games with." Then he was moving on, hustled along by his guide.

Kyle smirked. "You'll bring the frost if you anger the winter gods," he said. He urged them toward the door, reaching out his hand to lay it on Picket's shoulder. Picket shrugged it off.

"He's been promoted from winter king to winter god now?" Heather said. "That didn't take long. This equality you Terralains preach is really compelling."

"You don't know him," Kyle said, glancing back as his father shook hands with Captain Frye. "You are wrong to underestimate him."

"So we should think of him as an opponent?" Picket asked as they ducked through the door. Kyle followed them into the corridor.

"Of course not," he said. "Father liberated this place. He saved you all. He wants to liberate the world. He's not a winter god, of course, but he does not like defiance. I've had to do hard things," his head went down, "in the past."

"Will he settle for being our winter king?" Heather asked. "When the snow melts and Prince Jupiter Smalls returns, will the two of you stand aside? Or will you betray him again?"

Kyle looked away. He rubbed his eyes, ran his hands through his fur, and walked back toward the door. Finally, he turned to the Longtreaders. When he did, he looked tired. Deeply weary. Picket thought the mask was finally broken and they were seeing the real rabbit.

"Let Father be the winter king, Longtreaders," Kyle said. "We'll see what happens in spring. If it ever comes."

Chapter Eighteen

CARRIED OFF

Over the next week, the Silver Prince became the Winter King. He ruled Halfwind like a father to a thousand orphans. Heather watched Prince Bleston run the secret citadel uncommonly well, his fame growing with every new day. Heather was anxious and full of dread, but the new reality came on them like the winter snow—inevitable, unstoppable. Just as she couldn't make it autumn again, she couldn't alter the reality of life in the citadel.

Heather didn't see the falling snow, for she was inside, tending to her most urgent duties. Helmer's wounds kept him confined to the hospital, where she and Emma kept vigil over him to make sure he wouldn't leave before he was healed. No small task. And they had many, many more. Heyna Blackstar was also in the hospital, and she received Emma's tender attention as well. The beautiful young doe—whom Heather had disliked for no good reason—had come between the wolves and Emma, battling desperately. She had paid a high price for it. Her face bore an unmistakable mark from the battle, a scar she would carry with her for life. She would be a long time recovering.

There was always work, and little else, for Heather. She ate. She slept. At times, she and Emma laughed—silly, sleepless, survival laughter—then they carried on with their duty.

"Have you done Jo's wrap?" Emma asked, flitting from bed to bed and looking as exhausted as Heather felt.

"Not yet," Heather answered, digging in the satchel that had become like an extension of her body, she wore it so often. "After I dose the Willow twins, I'll redo it."

"It's been..?" Emma began, her face crunched in concentration.

"I think only a day," Heather said. "Maybe two?"

"It's only been a day," Jo Shanks said, raising his voice above the din. "You wrapped it yesterday, for some reason."

Emma whirled on him. "For some reason?" she said. He froze and his smirk disappeared. "I'll tell you why we clean and wrap your wound every day, Mr. Shanks. It's so it doesn't get infected and rot your arm off."

"I...I...didn't mean—" Jo began.

"If you want to have only one arm," Emma went on, "then sure, stop listening to your doctor and do whatever you want. I'm not sure you'll be quite as useful with that bow of yours, but by all means, ignore us. We're only doctors after all, not super-important Fowlers with urgent top-level elite work to do."

"I'm sorry, Doctor," he said. "You're right."

She eyed him coolly, finally turning back to Heather and winking.

Heather moved to the beds in the youngling section and carefully measured out a dose of Emma's prescribed tonic for each of the twins. She patted the young buck's head. These two, a brother and sister, were orphaned after losing their father in the battle. They were ill and had been in the hospital since before the battle.

"You'll be well again soon, Lukan. Doctor Emma has a tonic that's just what you need."

"Better than the potions in your stories?" he asked, coughing.

Heather leaned close so only the two of them could hear. "I think," she whispered, glancing side to side, "that she got it from a wizard. But don't tell anyone."

"Is that why it tastes so bad?" Lukan asked, sticking out his tongue. He continued in a conspiratorial whisper. "In stories, the magic tonics taste like sunlight and stardust. This medicine tastes like dirt-puddle and trash." Heather handed him his dose. He winced, gagged, then with a tremendous effort swallowed it down. "Yep. Dirt-puddle and trash."

"How do you know what—?" Heather began, but Lukan interrupted.

"Don't ask, Miss Heather," he said, raising his hand. "And I won't have to lie to you."

She nodded and turned to Elska. Concern filled her. "This will help you heal, Elska," she said. "Take it, dear child."

"Will it keep us from being carried away by the Preylords?" asked Elska. Her eyebrows furrowed and a pouty frown formed on her face. "They come for children, you know. The Preylords took Mamma. And they'll come for us."

"Nonsense," Heather said, crossing to sit beside her on the bed. "The Lords of Prey won't come in here. We have strong guards to block them, including my brother. He's a hero, you know."

"The wolves got in, Miss Heather."

"But we stopped them."

"Can your brother fight all the birds?" she asked. When Heather didn't answer right away, she nodded her little head. "I'll never go outside again," Elska said, and she swallowed her dose.

"If you can, Elska dear, think of happy things. The Mended Wood is coming, and we'll be free again."

The little doe lay down and pulled the covers up to her neck. "I don't want to be carried off. The Preylords come, and them they carry off, you never see again. I don't want to be carried off."

"Sleep, little one." Heather kissed Elska, smiled at Lukan, then crossed back to Jo, who was waiting by the door. She sighed, trying to turn her thoughts away from the intense needs of these little orphans. *And the others like them.*

"I didn't mean to insult you," Jo said, whispering as she drew near. "You of all rabbits. You saved my life on Cloud Mountain, and I'll never forget that."

"Emma's a little strained," Heather said, undoing the wrap on Jo's arm. As she began to clean the arrow wound, she went on. "I think we're all on edge. I blame exhaustion and the constant adjustments to new ways. And all the little tragedies," she said, glancing back at the twins.

"Has it affected you? The Silver Prince's new order, I mean. I thought you were kind of immune."

"No; it has," she said, beginning the new wrap. "The truth is, I'm in favor of almost everything he's doing to improve our preparedness. He's been a little hard, but I think we need it."

"He's a great leader," Jo said, nodding. "Lord Ramnor was a good rabbit, but he wasn't a military leader, really. Captain Frye made that side of things work, but not like the Silver Prince. He's a legend."

Heather nodded as she wound the wrap. "He's hard to resist."

"Resist?" Jo said. "Why should we resist him?"

"Because we already have a prince," she said, punctuating *prince* as she pulled the last of the wrap tight.

"Ow!" Jo said, wincing.

"Sorry," she said, adjusting the wrap. She patted his shoulder gently. "You may go, soldier."

He saluted and, after an awkward nod to Emma, left. Heather crossed to Emma, who was working at her desk alone. "Bleston's got Halfwind's heart in his hands," Heather said.

Emma looked up. "I hope he doesn't squeeze."

Chapter Nineteen

THE LAW OF THE SILVER PRINCE

H eather Longtreader, I have figured it out at last!"
The ancient creaking voice was familiar. Heather
turned to see Jone Wissel striding into the hospital, holding
aloft a small cinched purse. The purse was patchy and old,
with half-stitched holes and prominent stains. Its owner
was still more ancient. Jone was an enigma, disappearing
into the bowels of the Halfwind warren for months, then
emerging out of nowhere as if she'd never been absent.
Heather hadn't seen her in weeks.

"Aunt Jone!" Heather said, turning to face the bent old
rabbit, who leaned on a cane and looked up with wild eyes
and toothless gums. "It's been weeks since I've seen you. Are
you okay? Are you hurt at all?"

"I never hurt at all, Miss Longtreader!" Jone fairly shouted. Then she whispered conspiratorially, spitting
unwittingly as she did, "I did feel a bit down, but I dose
myself most precisely with all the precision of a white ant
crafting magnificent swords."

Heather raised her eyebrows, trying to work out the

meaning of Jone's word picture. But she stopped herself, remembering that Jone's metaphor puzzles were always difficult to crack. It was rumored that Jone had been the apothecary's assistant for many years but failed to get the post herself when her mother, Junie Wise, died. That was long ago, but no one knew precisely just how long ago. Lord Ramnor always said that Jone "came with the place," meaning she had been here long before he arrived.

"I'm so glad you're all right. You worry me, disappearing for weeks like that."

"Tut, tut!" Jone scolded. "You sound like an old hag. Naggy nag! Be free and happy, like a pickle in a pepper pot." She said this last while spinning a clumsy twirl. She finished the twirl by tripping and staggering sideways, and she only barely regained her balance by stabbing her cane into a passing soldier's foot. The soldier toppled, his foot still pinned, while Jone righted herself by leaning hard on her cane. Then she seemed to notice the buck, now in agony.

"Wah! I'm sorry, bucky!" she cried. "It appears," she went on, bending to whisper, and spit, near the crumpled soldier's ear, "that I've quite violently and egregiously pegged your poor foot." She examined his feet and noticed the other had already been bandaged. "It further appears," she said, resuming her shouting, "that this was the only foot you had in good working order. I beg you to forgive me, young'n. But I have a tonic that will set you up right away! Do I? I *do*!"

"Oh, Aunt Jone," Heather said, stepping in to help

the soldier up. "Remember, you agreed to let us do the doctoring. It's all right, Mitchell," she said to the groaning soldier. "Just lie back, and I'll have a look at your foot in a moment."

"He'll live," Captain Helmer said flatly, rolling over on his bed. He shot Mitchell a profoundly unsympathetic look.

"I'll be just fine," Mitchell said, smiling weakly as Jone patted his head a little harder than necessary. "Don't worry a moment, ma'am. I've had much worse."

Helmer nodded curtly, then turned back over with a rumbling mumble.

"He still needs a cure," Jone whispered close to Heather's ear. Heather blinked as the spittle flew, fighting off the urge to wipe her face every few seconds. She took Jone's arm in hers and led her gently toward the other side of the hospital, past the sleeping twins and the other younglings. They wound out into the broad hallway and stopped.

"How has your work been going?" Heather asked.

"I believe I've found it, at last!" Jone shouted, shaking the patchy purse in the air.

"Aunt Jone," Heather said gently, "I'm afraid you always say that."

"But this time—" Jone began.

"It's different," Heather finished. "Again."

"Ah," Jone said, touching her chin, "I take your point, reluctantly. I have said such things in the past."

"A few times," Heather said, taking her hand.

"I was saying it long ago," she said, her eyes growing suddenly dimmer. Heather thought she was seeing something like the old rabbit's real age now. "I have said it to a hundred young ones like yourself."

"I admire you for keeping after it. I really do."

Jone turned her suddenly tired eyes to Heather and squeezed her hand. "You are very kind, Heather," she said softly. "You have always treated me with a respect I'm sure I've never earned. Or, if I ever did earn it, it was a long time before you were even born."

Heather had never seen Jone act like this. It worried her. She seemed to fade before Heather's eyes, the wild light that energized her efforts dimming.

"What have you found, Aunt Jone?" Heather asked.

"Old Crone Jone!" A sharp shout came from the door. Heather turned to see Lieutenant Kout striding up, two guards flanking him. "You have been warned about getting into the prester's vault."

"Oh, Aunt Jone," Heather said, "what have you done?"

"It's not my fault that Kell's hoarding all the best supply!" Jone cried, eyes coming alive again as Kout's guards took her by the arms. "I needed the real thing for my tonic. He's got all the True Blue in this warren. I runned out a month back and haven't felt quite myself since."

"Gently, now," Heather said, reaching for their gripping hands. "Is this really necessary?"

"It's been too often, Heather," Lieutenant Kout said, shaking his head. "As forgiving as Prester Kell's been in the past, this ends now. King Bleston's system leaves no sympathy for thieves."

"What are you going to do for your 'King Bleston,' Lieutenant," Heather asked, "put her in jail?"

He sighed. "He's in command, Heather. And he is a king. As for Jone, she'll have to be confined. It's the law. No exceptions."

"Surely not," Heather said, coming close to Kout and whispering. "She could die in jail. Let me take care of her and I'll—"

"I'm sorry," he said, jerking his head to the guards. They pulled her away. He marched after them.

"Aunt Jone!" Heather cried. She couldn't let this be. She would go to Lord Ramnor—

But Lord Ramnor was dead. Smalls? He was gone. Lord Rake, Uncle Wilfred, and so many others she could turn to? All gone. Lord Ramnor would no more put Aunt Jone in prison than kick younglings. Angry and heart-heavy, she took a step toward the hospital door, but her foot kicked something. It slid across the floor in front of her, and she bent to retrieve it.

An old, patchy purse.

Heather picked it up. She smiled, shook her head, and shoved it into her satchel. Her face tightened again as she thought of how roughly they had handled poor old Jone.

"Emma!" she shouted, storming inside.

* * *

131

Picket watched Jo enter the noisy mess hall, wind his way through the line, and find a place beside the rest of the Fowlers. The hall was packed with soldiers now, most bearing the black and silver of Terralain. Perkinson was sitting beside Picket, and Coleden sat across from them both. Jo slid in beside Cole. Picket glanced at Jo's plate. Same as his plate. Short rations.

He longed for the Savory Den, for a cup of cider and some of that succulent soup, for an endless flow of honeyed bread. He wondered how Gort was faring, how all his friends on Cloud Mountain were getting along.

He thought of Mrs. Weaver, of how sad he had been to say goodbye to her. She had been a lifeline in a storm for him, a source of wisdom and acceptance he had never before known. The wise old rabbit would sew for hours and serve up counsel to small and great. Her wisdom was rooted in heartache, and she had understood Picket's pain. She had her own pain. Her husband had been carried off in the afterterrors, trading his life for hers. But to know her on Cloud Mountain had been a gift.

Picket had come back to life there. He missed the place but more so the many friends he'd left behind. There were others he missed, like Eefaw Potter and Doctor Zeiger. He hoped they were all safe. In some ways they were more vulnerable than Halfwind—an easier target, with so many civilians. Lord Rake had been slowly evacuating many of the families, but the truth was, there were few safe options.

Plans were still being made to send the most vulnerable

to Kingston. It was the safest place, but the journey was dangerous. He longed for a world where safe places for the weak and vulnerable were common, but that was not this world. Not right now.

Perkinson drained his cup and coughed, bringing Picket's attention back to the group.

"So we're all here," Perkinson said, speaking loud enough to be heard above the general clamor but quiet enough that only the Fowlers could hear him.

"Except for our master," Picket said.

"I guess you're it for us, now," Perkinson said. "Although I'm disappointed by how long it's taking you to hit us with a surprise attack. Personally, I'd suggest scalding us with this boiling, bitter, so-called 'coffee.'"

"I'd go for Jo's arm," Cole said. "He's sensitive there and has to get it wrapped by the pretty doctors every single day."

"Hey," Jo said, "they make me! It's not like I want to."

The Fowlers appeared unconvinced. "Of course," Perkinson said. "We never doubted you for a second, bucko."

"Listen up," Picket said. "I talked to Captain Frye about the messengers we sent to Kingston."

"No word?" Cole said, his smile vanishing.

"None."

"It's too early," Perkinson said. "The runners are fast, but not that fast."

"What about the envoy to Cloud Mountain?" Cole asked.

"Nothing there, either," Picket said, frowning.

"There was plenty of time for that route," Perkinson said. "It's not that far."

"I agree," Jo said.

"Maybe the wolves got them," Perk said. "Scouts are seeing wolves on the perimeter every day. It's just a matter of time before some break in to attack again."

"So what do we do?" Cole asked. "We need to get messages through."

"I'm thinking of going myself," Picket said. "I want to talk to Lord Rake."

"Will—" Perkinson began, but he stopped.

"Will the Silver Prince allow it?" Cole asked. "Is that what you're asking?"

"Yeah," Perkinson said. "There's a reality here we can't ignore."

"The reality that Bleston is in command?" Jo asked.

"Yes," Perkinson said. "That reality."

"I know," Picket said, "which is why I'm not going to ask."

"But he'll find out, Pick," Jo said. "He seems to know everything that's going on in this place before it even happens."

"He can't know," Picket said. "I've told almost no one. And anyway, I think I've slipped beneath the notice of the Silver Prince."

The large mess hall grew suddenly quiet. Picket looked up to see Kyle enter, accompanied by that massive captain, both in silver breastplates. On Kyle's other side stood an oddly dressed rabbit, old and robed in purple, his head dangling with beads and gems braided into his fur. He frowned as he scanned the room.

The hall was silent when the captain spoke. "Attention, soldiers! Prince Kylen has words." The soldiers from Terralain rose and stood at attention, followed by the Halfwind soldiers.

"Thank you, Captain," Kyle said, smiling and confident. This was the Kyle of old, poised and irresistibly charming. "My father invites the entire community to join him and Captain Frye in Leapers Hall at sundown tomorrow. Please dress in your best uniforms and be prompt. That is all." The soldiers of Terralain saluted.

"Sit," Kyle said, "enjoy your meals. You are all doing very well."

When the soldiers had resumed their seats and meals, Kyle left his companions at the door and made his way toward the Fowlers.

"What were you saying about going unnoticed?" Cole whispered.

"Picket," Kyle said, striding up, "Father wishes to speak to you."

Chapter Twenty

THE LORDS OF ALL WE SEE

Picket nodded to the other Fowlers and followed Kyle to the door.

"Picket," Kyle said, "I believe you know Captain Valter, one of our finest warriors."

"Captain Valter," Picket said, nodding.

"Lieutenant Longtreader," Valter said, returning the nod. The rabbit was nearly twice as tall as Picket. Muscles rippled beneath the fur on his arms and legs.

"And Tameth Seer," Kyle said, looking at the robed rabbit with jeweled fur and wild eyes. "May I introduce Lieutenant Picket Longtreader, the hero of the crossing and second in command of the elite Fowlers unit." Kyle turned to Picket. "Picket, this is Tameth Seer, Father's longtime advisor and friend."

"I am honored to meet you, sir," Picket said, bowing neatly.

"And I, you," the seer said, his voice high and brittle. "I have heard much of you, young Longtreader."

Picket felt uneasy. The ancient rabbit's gaze seemed to

penetrate his eyes and delve deep within him. "I see layers behind your eyes," the seer croaked. Then he spoke to Kyle as they walked. "I see a hinge for history in that one, Prince Kylen, much like I see in your father. And you."

Kyle nodded, and Picket walked on in silence. He had no idea what he was supposed to say. After a few more steps, Tameth Seer stepped in front of him, eagerly gazing into his eyes. Picket stood firm, tried not to blink. *I have nothing to hide.*

"I see you soar, Longtreader," he whispered, squinting as if trying to make out a distant shape. "I see you ascending."

Picket blinked, and the old rabbit blinked, and when he looked again, that mystical recognition was gone. He frowned, turning up the corner of his wrinkled mouth in some disgust. "What I might have seen, could I have looked but a little while longer. But now it is gone." He spat and walked on. The group re-formed behind him and moved forward.

In a few minutes, they reached the hallway before Bleston's receiving room, and the guards gave way before them, bowing to Kyle. They passed through, and Picket saw that up ahead Lieutenant Kout was bowing to Bleston. Kout was a good rabbit, one of Captain Frye's closest advisors. He ranked second only to Frye in Halfwind Citadel's army.

The lieutenant turned to leave, a smile on his face. The smile vanished when he saw Picket, and he nodded curtly as he passed.

"Longtreader, lad," the Silver Prince said, smiling wide, "I'm so glad to see you again."

"Prince Bleston," Picket answered, nodding.

Tameth hissed, and Picket saw Kyle shaking his head, but Bleston laughed. His laugh was like a wave crashing, like a rumbling thunder and sunlight in a meadow. Picket had never been in the presence of someone so energetic and compelling. He almost forgot his fear and spite in the warmth of that laughter.

"You remind me of your uncle," Bleston said. "He has that fantastic guile and snap."

"Uncle Wilfred?" Picket asked, but Bleston shrugged and went on.

"Longtreader, we must talk. I hear that you are gathering your own intelligence and have considered acting on your own instincts. Is this true?"

Picket tried to mask his surprise. *How can he know?* He glanced at the seer, saw that Tameth's penetrating gaze was fixed on him. *Can he really read my mind?*

"Sometimes," Picket began slowly, "we must take our own counsel and do what we deem best."

Bleston nodded. "I agree with you entirely. In your place, I would have done the same thing. I would seek to organize another mission to rescue my family. I would not wait for cautious ninnies to give permission."

Picket stared at Bleston, his mouth open. So this wasn't about the secret messengers between citadels. It was possible they had still gone undetected. Bleston was talking about his efforts to organize another attempt at rescuing his family.

"I did—that is, I *do* want to attempt a rescue," Picket said. He was about to say that he understood this goal must be subject to the needs of the army and the priorities of the war. But he didn't. Even when Bleston's silence left a long pause for him to fill, he didn't say it. The truth was, he was furious. He'd been seething about it, just under the surface, for months. He wanted nothing more than to do as he had vowed and rescue little Jacks and his parents. If Smalls had not tried it or had failed, he would go in a moment. But he didn't wish to defy the command structure.

"Has the mission been given a chance at all?" Bleston asked.

"Barely. We had one failed attempt, and the project was abandoned."

"The privileged lords didn't think it was best?"

"That's correct, sir."

"And the faulty intelligence came from…?" Bleston asked, eyebrows raised. Picket shifted his stance, looked down. "You don't have to answer me," Bleston went on. "I know what happened. But I must ask, do you share their opinion, Longtreader?"

"I…uh…well, sir…It's not my place…"

"Do you share their opinion?" Bleston asked again. This time his question carried an authoritative tone.

"No," Picket said. "I don't."

"Because you know that a small force, well-trained and well-prepared," Bleston said, "a small force like the Fowlers, could infiltrate one of the known slave mining camps. This force could rescue everyone there, returning soldiers to duty, reuniting families and gaining valuable intelligence, all while striking a blow to Morbin's side."

Picket was silent. He had used almost those exact words when pleading with Lord Ramnor, Lord Blackstar, and the others only a few weeks before. He nodded.

Bleston's smile was gone. In its place was a plain concern. "There comes a point when a rabbit must know his way and go his way, when he must break the shackles of tradition and be free. Am I not right to say so, Tameth?"

"Your Majesty is right," the old seer said, his eerie voice cracking. "Rabbits who wait for their betters to act ought to act better."

"There's a point of turning, Picket," Bleston said. "A point in a rabbit's life where he must wrestle free of minders and…" He looked at Tameth.

"And thus free his mind," Tameth finished. "Forever one a slave will be when never once he chooses *me*."

"Almost every good thing in my life has come from following my own way," Bleston said, touching the chain at his neck. Picket noticed a familiar but odd pattern on the back of the gem. "I became the king I was meant to be by following my own way, and I have raised my son to do the same."

"Yes, Father," Kyle said.

"We shall never defeat the Lords of Prey," Tameth said,

"until we see ourselves as the true lords and prey on them."

"Wouldn't that just be replacing tyrants?" Picket said, though he felt his resolve to resist weakening every moment.

"The world will be ruled, Picket," Kyle said, glancing up at the painting of Flint and Fay. It was one of the very few things from Lord Ramnor's rooms that had not been cleared out. "And it won't be ruled by the weak. We can only hope to be ruled by strong rabbits with courage and good hearts. Flint didn't wait to be ruled. He acted, and the Leaping reordered the world."

"And you, Prince Kylen, must be such a rabbit," Tameth said, wiping his mouth. "You are another Flint, uniting the world and creating a new reality."

Picket spared a moment to consider who might be Kyle's corresponding Fay, but he buried the thought.

"We are the lords of all we see," Bleston said, glancing at his son. "If only we will *grasp* it. If we wait for permission to act, it will be gone by the time we do."

"So what are you saying?" Picket asked. "That I should take a team and save my family, no matter what my masters say?" The thought felt wrong, but wrong in a way that thrilled him.

"The only master you have to worry about is telling you this," Bleston said, his easy smile returning. "You're a coward if you don't."

"But—" Picket began.

Bleston looked down at him, squinting. "You're not a coward, are you?"

Chapter Twenty-One

Sween and Stitcher

Sween huddled with ten other household slaves, listening to Gritch's orders for the day. She had spoken to only a few of them here, though she recognized many from Akolan. It was a cold, grey morning, and snow piled on the edges of the windows. No fires burned in the stage—the area where the slave activities were prepped as ordered by Gritch—but they blazed in Morbin's lair and the surrounding rooms.

"Can anyone sew?" Gritch asked, looking directly at Sween.

"I can," she said. "Though I paint better."

"There's no painting here," Gritch grumbled, "but there are uniforms that need mending, and I've been asked to pull someone to do the job. Stitcher needs help."

Melody spoke up. "I can sew. I sew like a maniac, I do. Stitcher, whoever that is, will be wildly impressed with my sewing skills."

"It's Sween's job," Gritch said. "I want *you* where I can keep an eye on you."

"I've already got a buck I'm betrothed to, Gritch," Melody said, winking at Sween, "but I'm flattered."

"You silly doe," Gritch snapped at her, "I want to keep you out of trouble. Any more sass from you and you're off. Working here is a privilege. I can send you down to the trash fields easily enough." He pointed to a door where all the garbage was sent down a long tube to pile up and rot in a plateau above Akolan. Melody bowed her head and chewed her lip.

"Don't," Sween whispered.

"Listen to Sween, Melody," Gritch said. "She knows how to stay alive. You have a child, don't you, Sween?"

"Children," Sween said, her voice barely audible.

"So don't be a fool," Gritch growled. "Follow Sween's example."

Melody nodded, keeping her head down so that Gritch couldn't see her defiant expression.

"Go ahead, Sween," Gritch said. "Marbole will take you."

Sween wound her way up to the platform above, to the slave's dock. Marbole, one of the old carrier birds, was waiting.

"Gritch said I'm supposed to help Stitcher with uniforms," she said.

The bird nodded, sighing as he moved forward. She held up her arms and he balanced on one foot, reaching to grip her with the other. He squeezed, though Sween had long since learned to empty her lungs before that came. She was pulled away and swept sideways into the air. Marbole soared up briefly, and Sween could see the sun, splintered rays darting through the clouds. He descended then, edging through a spiraling sprawl of forts and palaces, each less spectacular than the golden peak of Morbin's lair.

The lair was perched high in a pine forest atop the tallest peak of the High Bleaks. The long winding spiral of nests was a staggering spectacle. Beneath it all, in a sprawling pit, a massive maw cut from cold stone, lay the slave city of Akolan, Sween's present home. She saw it briefly through a break in the trees before Marbole dipped and docked at another nest, spilling Sween roughly onto a wooden floor.

"Thank you," she said as the big bird beat his retreat. She got to her feet slowly, dusting her dress, and walked gingerly to the only rabbit on the dock. The hangar clerk. She was short, middle-aged like Sween, and sitting at a lonely desk before a large door.

"Yes?" the rabbit asked, eyes closed.

"I was sent here by Gritch, master slave of Morbin's—"

The small rabbit cut her off. "I know who Gritch is."

"I'm supposed to help Stitcher."

"Help Stitcher?" she asked, her eyebrows arching.

"That's what Gritch said."

The rabbit wrote in her ledger and spoke without looking up. "Down the hall, pass seven lefts and take the eighth, then pass five rights and take the sixth. If you hit the laundry, you've gone two lefts too far. If you hit the flaxery, you've taken three too many rights. Clear?"

"I feel like I've lost my rights," Sween said, smiling.

"Be glad of what's left," the small rabbit replied, without a hint of humor. "It can be taken away easily enough."

Sween was chilled by the reply. This humorless retort summed up the slave's dilemma. *Shouldn't we simply settle for what we have, be grateful we're even alive, and do our best to stay that way? Maybe she's right.*

Sween nodded and entered through the door. After getting mixed up a few times and finding help from friendlier rabbits, she knocked, then entered what she had been assured was Stitcher's room.

Inside, a small rabbit sat stitching a red vest. He kept at his work while Sween hesitated, astounded at the organized stacks of uniforms, capes, vests, and other clothes on shelves surrounding the room. Without looking up he asked, "What may I do for you?"

"I was sent here," she answered. "I'm a house slave from Morbin's lair."

"Is that really what you are?" he asked.

"Gritch said you needed help."

"No, I don't need help, ma'am." He smiled up at her. He was old and worn, but his eyes were kind. "I could stitch and sew ten times as fast as I do. I could make near-perfect uniforms. Instead, I make sure one in every twenty or so will come unstitched at what I hope are the most inopportune times."

Sween smiled nervously. "Don't you worry about talking like that to a stranger? I could be an informant."

He looked into her eyes and smiled again. "The dock clerk is an informant. You're not an informant. I could see that a thousand miles away. I can read rabbits. Not quite the way my wife can, no. But I can see what sort of rabbit you are. Besides, I know you."

"You do?" Sween asked. "Then you have me at a disadvantage. I don't know you."

"My name is Edward," he said, bowing his head slowly, then looking up at her again with a warm smile, "Edward Weaver."

"If you don't need help, Mr. Weaver, and you already know who I am, why did you want me to come?"

The old rabbit laid aside his stitching. "Because," he said, "I want to hear you sing."

Chapter Twenty-Two

A SMALL THAWING

Heather gripped her staff, driving it into the ground with every hurried stride she made. Emma had ordered her to take a walk and try to clear her head. She walked fast, unable to slow her mad pace, even on an ordered break. But after a few minutes her stride eased, her heart settled, and she began to breathe a bit easier.

Emma. Always with the right dose of the proper medicine. She walked the grounds outside Halfwind, absently winding through the twisted thorn passages.

She had not been at Halfwind long, but still she had fond memories. In this corner, she had walked with Smalls. She could almost see him there, smiling, waiting for her. In spite of the many demands on his time and attention, he had always found time for her. She missed him. She worried about him, intensely at times. That old fear she felt the day he left had lingered in her heart. Would he ever return? She longed for it. Not only for herself but for everyone who hoped for the Mended Wood. What they needed now was leadership, a strong, unifying figure to lead them in this war.

She walked through the outer gate and into the open ground surrounding the warren. There were guards patrolling, their breastplates bright, and other rabbits lingering. A knot of rabbits gathered near an oak that had become a makeshift memorial to the Silver Prince's rescue. There were notes of thanks, tokens of remembrance, and other humble odes to Bleston. The Bleston Tree, as the oak was now called, was near the place where he had defeated the wolves and where the soldiers of Halfwind, with a streaming crowd from the citadel, had surrounded and cheered him in his incredible victory. Heather had been inside when it happened, but all those who recounted the scene spoke of it reverently, cheerfully. Some wept. In the weeks following there had even been songs composed, and the halls rang with singing rabbits, honoring the Silver Prince.

Heather watched as the group of rabbits laid their small tributes, their gifts to the Lord of Terralain. Then they knelt—actually knelt—beneath the oak. They kept a somber silence for a long while. Heather watched, a frown slowly forming on her face.

"You're prettier when you smile," someone said. For a moment her heart leapt, for the voice was familiar, and it took her back to Cloud Mountain. She turned to see Kyle, an apologetic smile on his face. She frowned. "You're disappointed to see me," he said.

"You're as perceptive as you are deceptive," she answered. His face went down. She felt a stab of guilt. Should she let the past go? After all, hadn't he done enough in rescuing her, Emma, Picket, everyone here, to warrant a civil reply? "I'm sorry, Kyle."

"No, you must not apologize," he said. Gone was the guile and charm. In its place was a weary sadness. "I deserve it. You could never reproach me as much as I reproach myself."

"You regret it?" she asked.

"Deeply, Heather," he said. He came to stand beside her. "You cannot imagine how much. I wish Smalls were here so I could apologize to him. It's just...I was...it simply got out of hand."

She chose her words carefully. "I'm sure the future king would forgive you."

"May I walk with you?" he asked. She nodded, and they moved through the clearing and into a trail in the woods. For a while they said nothing. The only sounds were their footfalls and Heather's staff tapping the ground. She moved toward the Fowlers' course, but he took another path, and she, after hesitating a moment, followed.

"Where are we going?" she asked. She almost said, *Not into a trap, I hope,* but she held her tongue.

"I've been talking with Father. I know you have wise words for him, about Smalls, about this place. I want you to have a chance to talk to him, to advise him, without all the pomp of his receiving room."

"So you're taking me to meet him in the forest?"

"Yes. But only if you're comfortable with it. I hoped

it would be a chance for you to meet him away from the ceremony of his court."

She nodded and they walked on. "I don't know what you hope to accomplish."

"I just want you to talk to him," Kyle said. He started to go on but clamped his mouth shut again, looking away.

"What is it?"

"Well, I'm reluctant to advise you, Heather. But if you'll allow a small caution."

"You want me to bow and scrape to the self-appointed king of all Natalia? I'm sorry, Kyle. I have to tell the truth."

"Could you call me Kylen?" he asked. "It is my name, after all. And Kylen's story is the one I love. Kyle's—well, you know how that went."

"All right, Kylen."

"Thank you," he said. "About Father. I wouldn't ask you to lie or to hold back from speaking your mind. I only want you to give Father a chance. He's capable of listening. If you think him totally unreasonable, then you'll be likely to burst out and insult him."

"As Picket and I have done?"

"Well, yes. He respects your passion. But I would advise you to make your case. Try to persuade him. Don't despair and resort to barbs. You have a chance to be heard, Heather. I've seen to that. Don't waste it."

They walked in silence for a time, and the snow began to fall again. There was no wind. The flakes fell slow and steady, soft, wet petals dropping from a hidden glade in the clouds.

"Thank you, Kyle," she said. "Kylen," she corrected. They walked on, farther and farther from the trails surrounding the citadel.

"I'm not your enemy," Kylen said. "I hope one day you'll know that for sure."

"I hope so too."

He reached for her hand, but she drew it back. "I'm sorry," he said. "I only mean to offer my friendship to you and Picket. I hope you'll give me another chance."

She thought of her brother, of how unlikely it was he would ever be able to forgive Kylen. Should she forgive him? Emma never would. And that was without her even knowing that Smalls was her brother.

"We'll have to see what can happen over time," she said, smiling as kindly as she was able. He reached for her again, his eyes wide. Her smile disappeared and a scowl replaced it, but he grabbed her and threw her to the ground with a shout.

She hit the ground hard and rolled. She cried out and looked up to see a wolf charging from the woods.

Chapter Twenty-Three

WHO'S THE TRAITOR?

Kylen leapt in front of Heather, his hand going to his sword. She panicked, knowing he would not draw it in time.

He didn't.

The wolf pounced on Kylen. Heather sprang up, crying for help. She hoped the Silver Prince was nearby. She scanned the forest, seeing no one. Nothing.

She spun back and saw Kylen's face awash in terror, his eyes wide and his mouth open in a pained cry. The wolf was latched onto his shoulder and had him pinned to the ground. Kylen's free hand still sought the hilt of his sword, but he couldn't reach it. *This will be over in seconds,* Heather thought.

She charged the wolf, knowing only that she couldn't stand by and let Kylen die. She closed the gap in seconds, coiled for a kick, and launched, landing her powerful feet in turn—right, with a crash, then left, with a resounding smash!—on the wolf's head. He fell back, shaking his head in shock.

Heather tumbled to the ground beside Kylen. She rose quickly, reaching for the wounded rabbit. The wolf was on his feet again, slavering jaws wide, eyes burning.

"Your choice," he snarled. "Death…or death?"

She planted her feet in front of Kyle. "I choose death," she said coldly, "for you and your wicked masters."

The wolf howled, a frenzy seizing him so that he shuddered with delight.

Then he ran at her. It couldn't have lasted more than a few seconds, but she saw it all in frozen moments. His eyes. Cruel eyes. Wild with excitement. Mad with hunger. Closing to thin slits, keen in attack. Coming. Close. Closer still. Then opening wide in surprise.

The wolf was lurching back, staggering, collapsing on the forest floor.

Kylen had reached around her, his sword standing between the wolf and his prey. Between her and death. At the last possible moment, he had acted.

She turned to him, her eyes wide. He fell back. Dropping his sword, he clutched his torn shoulder. Then his hand went limp, his eyes closed, and he sank to the earth. He didn't move.

She knelt beside him, her hand going to the wound to try to stop the bleeding. She heard noises behind her, and in a moment they were surrounded by soldiers, including several Terralain field medics. Heather backed away as they swept in, nearly tripping over the wolf. She turned and ran into the woods, frantic. She stopped beneath a towering

oak and fell to her knees, and the tears came.

For a long time she sat there, shivering. Finally, she heard a voice from behind.

"Are you all right, Heather?"

She turned to see Bleston, his face full of concern. "Is he—?" she asked.

"He'll recover," he said. "He comes from a strong family."

"He saved me," she said, rubbing her eyes. "The wolf would have…he was nearly…"

"There, there, child," he said, wrapping her in a fatherly embrace. "I know. I know."

They stood in silence awhile, Heather feeling comforted as she hadn't been in a long time—since her own father had held her long ago and told her everything was going to be all right.

* * *

Picket found Captain Frye on Westfield, reviewing the training exercises led by his sub-captains and lieutenants. All the officers, including Frye, wore the sign of the blood-red moon, with a ruby in the center of crossed spears. Along the path to the gates of Leapers Hall, rows of archers aimed and released their arrows in time with their officers' calls. Hay bales bristled with arrows, and the air was filled with urgent instruction from all corners of the wide field. Marching bands of armed rabbits paraded the perimeter while new recruits struggled through an endurance course.

Near the woods, blue-robed brothers worked with soldiers to complete the construction of three large wheeled catapults. One looked near working order, and they seemed to be prepping a trial with a large barrel. Picket noticed Heyward among those votaries aiding the construction. The field was full of white-clad soldiers, their shoulders bearing the symbol of the blood moon, the crossed spears. Black-clad officers from Terralain stood nearby, wordlessly watching.

Captain Frye glanced back and forth from the glowering guests to his army in the field. Picket scowled. Captain Frye had always been strident about his army's capability. But that was before they had to be rescued by warriors fighting beneath a black banner with silver stars. He was reserved now, tenuous. He was not quite himself.

"Captain Frye," Picket said, trotting up.

"Yes, Lieutenant?"

"May I have a word?"

"Now?" he said. He met Picket's gaze and saw the urgency in his face. "Sure, son. Of course. Walk with me." They walked together down the slight sloping hill and around the near perimeter of the snowy field. "What can I do for you, Picket?"

"I'm planning a mission to the prison camp," Picket said. "I'll take the Fowlers and make a surgical strike, recovering our prisoners and gathering useful intelligence. I wanted you to know."

Captain Frye stopped, sighed, and rubbed his eyes. "Did the Silver Prince tell you that your family was there?"

"No, sir."

"Your own network then? How many factions must we have in this war?" He clenched and unclenched a tight fist. "We weaken the bridge when we splinter into bits."

"It wasn't my own network, sir. I don't have a network. I've been on your side, following you, throughout."

"And yet you come to me, your superior officer, and you tell—not ask, mind you—you tell me you are going on a raid and taking valuable assets into an incredibly dangerous and reckless situation?"

Picket looked down, anger simmering. "It was Smalls who told me. And I can't believe it's an impossible task. We are trained for—"

"Training, son," Captain Frye said. "You are training. Not trained."

"So you want us to do nothing?" Picket said. His resentment over this old argument was flaring up again.

"No, son. I don't want us to do nothing. I want us to do nothing *alone*. Nothing out of anger, guilt, or tactical folly. I want *us* to win this war. Do you know how many campaigns I've planned? Do you know how many battles I've fought? Do you know how many raids I've taken part in—how many 'can't fail' and 'surgical' strikes I've been a part of? Do you know, Picket?" Picket looked away. "More than none, Picket, which is where you and I are different."

When Picket looked up, he expected to see anger in his captain's eyes. But Frye looked old and weary as he went on. "I wish Prince Smalls had not mentioned it to you. All the military minds in his council advised him to avoid the slave mine site. Old campaigners from King Jupiter's wars, lords and captains loyal in the darkest hours of these last bleak years, all argued against it. Not one disagreed with this, though the prince himself argued for making a detour to liberate the camp. I think it was out of love for your sister and gratitude to you. But no one endorsed his plan. In the end, I hoped we convinced him. Only a fool would advise him otherwise. As I advised him, my superior, so I order you, a soldier in my army, against this folly. You might succeed, Picket. But the cost, I fear, would be greater than whatever was won. That is, unless you care about nothing more than this one objective. If you care about the cause, the war, the prince…do not do this foolish thing."

Picket didn't know what to say. His anger was ebbing away, replaced by a brewing dread. Should he tell Captain Frye what he had done, that he had advised the prince to attack the camp?

"Captain Frye," came a shout from the field. A band of soldiers stood at attention. "We are ready for you, sir." He nodded and held up a finger, then turned back to Picket.

"I'm for you, Picket. And I'm for your family. I feel terrible regret that my failure led you to the wrong camp those months ago. I do. I feel your frustration now. But son, there's a war coming to us, a war unlike anything any of us have ever experienced—even those of us who have been through wars before." He placed a hand on Picket's shoulder. "Bleston was a rabbit who went his own way. Your Uncle Garten was like that. You are not like them, Picket. And whatever part of you is sympathetic to that path is a part of you that's best buried in the deepest, darkest tomb, like Lander's dragons. For all our sakes."

Captain Frye patted Picket's arm, then hurried toward his waiting army. Picket stood there, rising dread forming knots in his stomach. But his reverie was soon broken by a commotion in the forest. Rabbits were shouting and running back and forth. Sentinels ran toward Captain Frye and the Terralain officers.

It took him several minutes to learn that Heather had been attacked in the woods. Prince Kylen, now badly wounded, had saved her. Picket was relieved to learn that Heather was all right. Thinking of Kyle's acts and his own conversation with Smalls, he began to wonder if he had a right to resent Kyle at all.

Who had done more damage? Who was the hero, and who the traitor?

Chapter Twenty-Four

THE KING OF TURNS

Heather finished wrapping Kylen's shoulder and gave him a large dose of Emma's tonic. He drank it without opening his eyes. Bleston sat beside his son's bed, intent on everything she did.

"This tonic is good," Heather said, checking Kylen's pulse. "Emma developed it in her training years along with an old doctor on Cloud Mountain. Despite what I tell the younglings, it's not magic. But, with some sleep and proper care of his wounds, we'll see him recover in time."

"Thank you, Heather," Bleston said. "I appreciate you coming to his room like this. We have good healers in Terralain, but I have heard amazing things about your team since the battle."

"It's Emma's team," she said. "And the recovery times have improved, I'll admit. I think it's mostly due to Emma's leadership. She's done for Halfwind's medical team something like what you've done for military discipline." She bit her lip, debating whether or not to bring up Jone's case. *Not yet.*

"I believe the prince is in very good hands," Bleston said. "We are grateful for your service to him."

"Well, sir, Kylen did save my life," she said, placing several vials and a bolt of cloth into her satchel.

Bleston smiled. "There is something I wish to discuss with you, child."

"Yes, sir?" she said, setting down her bag.

"Kylen has been speaking to me about you. He believes I should listen to your advice, that I should turn to you for wisdom. I am almost convinced he is right."

"Well, sir," she said, taking the offered seat beside him, "Kylen believes you are a great king, truly capable of listening and willing to change your mind if confronted with the truth."

"I hope I always am, child."

"Well, lord, may I ask how you see things now?"

Bleston smiled at her. "I am inclined, dear Heather, to be entirely truthful with you."

"Then I'm honored, lord."

"Not that I speak falsehoods, but I must keep much of my own counsel bottled up. It's the burden of a king. It will be good to discuss these heavy things with someone I trust."

"Thank you, sir."

"I can trust you, can I not?" he asked.

"I will hear you with humility," she said, touching her ears. Then, touching her eyes, she said, "I will see you with generosity." Finally she touched her mouth. "And I will speak to you with honesty."

"It is well, child. Very well. It's good that you honor the old ways." Bleston sat awhile, his eyes closed and his mouth tight. At last, he spoke again. "I am in a difficult place, but a place of power. I am, I suppose, the king of turns. I am the lord of the balance. If I tip to Morbin—which is not in my heart to do—he rules all. If I tip to my brother's young upstart son, he has a chance to rule all. But I do not see myself as a traitor, only a maker. I see myself as the wielder of worlds, the one who fashions fortunes. I am the magnetic heart of Natalia, drawing all to myself."

"But you have no designs on the throne yourself?" she asked, eyebrows raised.

"I would like to be king of Natalia, as I have a plain claim to the throne and the Whitson Stone to witness to my rights. I also have the strength to take it and the will to keep it."

"But you don't want this?"

"I want it for one thing," he said, nodding to the bed. "So that I might give it to Kylen."

Heather frowned. "Speak, child," Bleston said. "Be bold."

"I will speak boldly and plainly, sir." She drew in a deep breath and went on. "I think you're right about yourself. You are the king of turns, a mover of worlds. So, move to the straight path. You're a kingmaker, so make Smalls what he deserves to be. Show yourself truly great and make him your king. Do what you never did for his father, your brother. Honor him. Honor the choice your father made and the choice your brother, King Jupiter, himself made. Throw your support behind your nephew, and you will live with an acclaim unmatched in history. Be the bold and selfless uncle. Be the true kingmaker, and make the true heir king."

"My, but you are bold, little one," he said, shaking his head. Before she could speak again, he held up a hand. "I have heard you, Heather Longtreader. I *can* listen. I am... sorry about what happened with my brother. I would like to make it right. Many times I have wished I could have been there when he was betrayed and murdered at the crossing." He shook his head. "But I will be an old rabbit soon. I have others to think of," he said, glancing again at Kylen.

"Think of *all* the sons, lord. Think of all the huddled, hurting ones living under oppression, longing for the Mended Wood."

"You are their scribe, are you not? How well you love them."

"I'm only a herald, like thousands beside me," Heather said. "But we all sing the same song. Things are bad, yes. But it will not be so in the Mended Wood."

"I have heard this song."

"Sing it with us, Lord Bleston," she said. "Lend your strong voice and hasten its coming. Be for us always the Silver Prince, who rides in to rescue, who helps make a truly noble rabbit our longed-for king."

Bleston looked away, blinking. He swiped his forearm across his eyes and then looked back at Heather.

"And you, my dear? What will you be?"

"I want to be a queen," she said, without hesitation.

"What a grand one you'll be, to be sure."

"I want to listen to my stories again and hear my mother sing. I want to see my little brother grow up free."

Bleston nodded. "These are good dreams, I think."

"You will consider my plea, lord?"

He nodded, looking very grave, then motioned toward the door.

She stood and knelt before him. Then she rose, grabbed her satchel, and moved quietly to the door. Before she left, she looked back. Bleston had his head in his hands.

As she hurried to the hospital, something stirred in her that had long been still. Hope.

Perhaps I am the queen of turning? For my dear prince's sake, and for the sake of the whole wounded world, may it be so.

Chapter Twenty-Five

EVERY STEP ON THESE
SILVER STAIRS

I didn't know who else to talk to." Picket sat on the floor of Leapers Hall, beneath the third of the seven standing stones that split the center of the massive hall. They were alone in the great chamber, and Heyward settled onto the hard floor across from Picket, his blue robe draped over his knees.

"I'm only a novice," he said, putting down his knife and a small box-shaped contraption, "but I'm always here for you, my friend."

"I think I made a great mistake," Picket said. He told Heyward about his last conversation with Smalls and about what Captain Frye had said to him. Heyward nodded, his face grave. Picket concluded his story with tears pooling in his eyes. "What if I've done it? What if I've placed such a heavy burden of guilt on Smalls that he does this foolish thing? What if I've played on his loyalties and loves, encouraging him to make a disastrous move?"

"Picket, I have listened to you. You speak humbly, contritely. Beneath the standing stones honoring our ancestors, this is fitting. Now, by Flint, I give you bold words. By Fay, words of wisdom. By all the Leapers, I speak the truth. You may indeed have erred when you advised the prince to liberate the camp. It appears you have. But the prince is…well, he's the prince. He is responsible for the actions he takes. You are not." Picket made to interrupt, to object, but Heyward held up a hand. "Listen, Picket. Prince Smalls was responsible for his decision when he followed Kyle's advice and went to Jupiter's Crossing. You were responsible for your decision when you followed him there and saved his life."

"But, Heyward," Picket said, wringing his hands. "I knew the best counsel for him, and I undermined it by manipulating his heart. I'm more like Kyle at Cloud Mountain than me at Jupiter's Crossing."

"Not true, Pick. There is an enormous difference."

"I can't see it," Picket said.

"Yours was advice based on hope and love," Heyward said. "Kyle's was cold and calculating, given with ill intent."

"I'm not sure he would see it that way, Heyward. He would say he did it for the greater good and that he was only obeying his father."

"It's not the same, Picket. You weren't motivated by power or compulsion but by love and loyalty."

"I'm afraid," Picket said, getting to his feet, "that both of us were motivated by our fear and pain."

"Try to enjoy the assembly tonight," Heyward said, reverently touching his ears, his eyes, and his mouth, "and forget your woes. Hopefully the prince listened to his best advisors and bypassed the camp. We can all pray that he's safe and strong and on his way to Kingston now."

"By the Leapers," Picket said, glancing around, "I hope so."

* * *

Heather gazed around Leapers Hall as the room steadily filled. The walls were a mixture of rock and clay, with great iron gates on the side leading out to Westfield. Beyond the gates stood a series of heavy doors, all hidden from outside by clever means. She hoped they would never have to flee a cave-in by that route and that no enemy would ever somehow enter there.

The floor of the hall was laid with stones, and the wooden stage was high. The center of the stage was raised even higher, and it was made of a large grey stone. In front of this central stone, extending out into the hall, were seven standing stones. These were surrounded by blue-robed votaries, who sat reverently beneath them, heads bowed, with whispered words on their lips.

Heather and Picket had been raised to appreciate the Leaping and to revere Flint and Fay. But here, the devotion was intense and intentional. In fact, she had always thought of Flint and Fay like the first in a long line of heroes. In Cloud Mountain it was much the same, though there were few votaries there during their stay. She had heard that devotion had grown in the days since her story of Picket and Smalls had been shared. Lord Rake had said that Cloud Mountain's seven standing stones, once neglected, in a secluded area past the village green were now visited by growing numbers of devoted rabbits. Here at Halfwind, Flint and Fay were more than old heroes to be admired. They were holy ancestors, touched by divinity.

She found a place near the base of the seventh standing stone and looked around for Emma and Picket. When she saw them, she waved to get their attention. Soon they all found a place in the shadow of the seventh stone where they could see the stage.

As the crowd grew and settled in, Emma spoke quietly. "I passed the Silver Prince's receiving room on the way here," she said. "I couldn't see much, but I overheard arguing. He and his creepy advisor, that Tameth Seer character, were shouting at each other."

"Shouting?" Heather asked. "I can't imagine anyone shouting at Bleston."

"Exactly. Not if they value their lives," Emma said. "He cultivates a jovial image, but it's easy to see that beneath it he's deadly serious. He gets his way, or there's a storm. I sensed that right off."

"If anyone could argue with him," Picket said, "it would be Tameth. He's been Bleston's counselor for years."

"Maybe Bleston's going to do something he wasn't planning to do," Heather said, hopeful.

"I don't like it," Emma said. "It felt so strange."

"These are strange days," Picket said. "Who knows what to expect? Like tonight. What are we doing here?"

"Bleston called an assembly," Emma said. "He's the ruler of this citadel now, and I think he wants to consolidate his power."

"But don't the votaries lead all gatherings here?" Heather asked.

"They do," Emma answered. "But they don't make military policy. In the past, they've always handed over the stage to Lord Ramnor. Tonight could be interesting."

As she spoke, the senior votaries filed in two by two and mounted the steps leading up to the high stage. Reaching the top, they fanned out across the wide platform. The master votary, Prester Kell, and his wife, Sage Kins, came last of all. They stood in the middle, hand in hand.

A thumping music struck up, pensive and loud. Votaries waved branches over the wall lamps, casting eerie shadows over the hall. The music intensified as those on stage bent and bowed, making slow, solemn motions that signified tremendous upheaval.

Heather glanced around, noticing the rabbits of Terralain. For once, they were alarmed. Their eyes bulged as they felt for their swords.

The music built to a fever pitch, and the votaries crashed to the platform. Then Prester Kell and Sage Kins rose solemnly. A light burst behind them, and they seemed to glow. Hands still clasped, they moved slowly to the edge of the stage. Drums thundered, the votaries roared, and the broken light made baneful shadows dance around the room.

When Heather thought she could endure no more, the music suddenly stopped. Together, Kell and Kins leapt to the first standing stone. As they launched, the music returned, this time harmonious and bright. Trumpets blasted a happy anthem, joined by strings and voices singing in harmony. The chimes built up until they leapt in time with the trumpet's two-note refrain.

The chief votary and his wife landed on the second standing stone, their feet hitting as a hail of cymbals crashed. This was repeated again and again until they reached the sixth standing stone. Heather, Picket, and Emma gazed up at them along with the rest of the rapt, expectant crowd.

They leapt to the trumpet's call and landed with a crash of cymbals and the thunder of drums. Finally the music resolved in a melody Heather felt she must have heard before.

When the music ended, there was silence. Kins sat on the seventh stone, and everyone, starting with the votaries, followed her lead and sat.

Prester Kell touched his ears, his eyes, his mouth. As he did so, he sang, and though no instruments accompanied this song, most of the assembly joined in. "Let us hear with humility, see with generosity, speak with honesty, and so leap with audacity!" Prester Kell nodded, then held up his hand, turning slowly in a circle as he spoke.

"Gathered exiles of the Mended Wood. Children of blessed Flint and Fay, greetings. I speak to you today from the seventh standing stone. Why? It is for this reason, my friends. The seventh stone is a stone of turning. We know what happened on the sixth stone. We know the Wind Hook well. But the seventh stone is where Flint and Fay could have turned back. This is where they paused, turned, and saw what was behind them. This is where their final decision was made. Would they turn back and return to the life they knew, back on Immovable Mountain? Or would they go on, becoming they knew not what in a land they could not hope to understand? Their dreams were not guides but visions of what could be. This is where they turned and turned again and leapt at last into a new world."

Heather sat taller, her gaze following the blue-robed prester as he circled above her.

"What would we do, faced with such a decision? Would we leap? I don't know what I *would* have done. I only know what I *will* do. In this moment—and every moment is a new Leaping in miniature—I will do what our ancestors did. I will leap. And leap, and leap again!"

The crowd clapped and the music began again as the assembly rose to cheer the prester. Kell bowed low, then drew Sage Kins to her feet and raised his hand for silence. He and Kins began to sing. Soon, the whole assembly joined in.

"Bring us out of this mountain of doom,
Our upturned world of woe,
Take us leap by leap, by leap, along,
To glories yet unknown.

Every step on these silver stairs,
Over ancient abysmal heights,
Brings us closer to Blue Moss Hills,
Out of darkness and into the light.

The Immovable Mountain heaved,
And from stone to stone we soared.
By Fay's stone book we look and see,
And we live by Flint's stone sword.

We go on with grateful hearts,
For this inheritance so kind,
Our fathers dreamed, believed, and leapt,
So we that we, one day, might fly."

When the song was done, Prester Kell turned toward the stage. "My dear friends," he said. "Let us welcome one whom you all know. He has been for us a light in the darkness, a hook of wind on our sixth step. He has been a gift of life. I invite Prince Bleston, king of Terralain, to speak to us all in this hallowed place."

The applause came like thunder, and Heather turned to see the Silver Prince, flanked by a spectacularly decorated honor guard, making his way up the steps to the stage. The crowd roared and sprang to their feet. Heather stood with them, feeling a growing sense of dread.

When at last the crowd was quieted, Bleston spoke. Heather reached out for Emma's hand and clasped it tight.

"Thank you, friends," Bleston said, "for your kind welcome, both to me and to my fellows. First of all, some things need to be made clear. Heather and Picket Longtreader, please come forward and join me."

Heather was alarmed, and she saw that Picket was frowning. Reluctantly letting go of Emma's hand, she made her way toward the stage alongside her brother. "My dear friends, I give you the hero of Jupiter's Crossing and the Scribe of the Mended Wood!" The crowd cheered, and many rabbits reached out to touch them as they passed.

They climbed the stairs. When they reached the platform, Bleston embraced them. "Now," Bleston continued, "there's another rabbit who needs to be up here." The crowd quieted as Heather's heart raced. She clung to Picket's arm. Bleston looked down at the foot of the seventh stone. "Emma," he said. "Please join us."

Frowning, and through a smattering of applause,

Emma slowly made her way toward the stage. Picket shot a panicked glance at Heather. She stepped forward and tried to speak to Bleston, but he motioned for her to step back.

Turning to the crowd as Emma reached the platform, Bleston spoke in slow, serious tones. "I'm afraid Emma has a secret."

THE WHITSON STONE

Bleston put his arm around Emma. Heather gasped. She caught a glimpse of Captain Frye, his eyes wide as he stepped forward.

"Our Emma is much more than the quiet healer she seems to be," Bleston said.

"Do something," Heather whispered to Picket.

Picket looked from Heather to Bleston, uncertain what to do. He spread his hands, palms up. Heather looked back at Emma, saw her confusion and embarrassment.

"I'm very happy to announce," Bleston said, his smile wide and his voice like gold, "that Emma has—quietly and humbly—improved the results of our medical unit beyond anything I have ever seen, even in peacetime."

Heather almost collapsed with relief. Picket sagged as well, his hands moving to smooth the fur on his ears.

"I've seen her team in action, and thanks in no small part to her, my son, Prince Kylen, is recovering." The crowd cheered once more, and Picket leaned close to his sister.

"That was close," he said. "But why does he have us up here?"

Bleston raised his hands, and the crowd slowly quieted. "My friends, I have invited these representatives of this community to join me on stage so I could make an announcement. A hero," he said, motioning toward Picket. "A poet," he said, smiling at Heather. "A healer," he said, bowing to Emma. "These excellent rabbits are just some of the wonderful young friends I've met since returning to the world outside of Terralain. They give me hope. You, all of you, give me hope.

"I was born and raised in the First Warren. I was the oldest son of my father, strong and fully qualified to be his heir. When I left I took the token of my birthright." Here he reached into his shirt and lifted the golden chain bearing the large bright ruby. "This stone, known in my ancestor Whitson's time as the Ruling Stone, has been the symbol of legitimate authority in Natalia since our earliest days."

Heather frowned. She didn't like where this was going. "The owner of the stone was by rights the ruler of all Natalia. Though for a season I sojourned in another land, I have never abandoned that responsibility. And now Natalia and Terralain are united in purpose and in leadership."

A soft murmuring rippled through the crowd. Heather could see that she and Picket weren't the only ones who'd caught the scent of treason. Should she make a heroic stand and defy Bleston? Should she attack him? She listened warily with an undisguised frown.

"Together, we will forge a new alliance and oppose Morbin's lordship. We will restore the Great Wood to the rightful rule of rabbits. We will drive out the usurpers. Until then, we must oppose those of royal blood who have become obstacles to our cause."

Heather's worry hardened into anger. She saw that Picket's hands were balled into fists and his right hand rested on the pommel of his sword, worn at his side tonight.

The crowd grew more anxious as Bleston continued. "My brother's son rules the First Warren as a puppet governor for Morbin," he said, and Heather relaxed a moment. That was Smalls' oldest brother, Winslow. "He must be routed out. Winslow oversaw the building of the wall. He ordered the burning back of the perimeter. He makes certain no word goes in or comes out. I have learned that they do great evil there, that raptor sentinels sit on the walls and swoop in to steal younglings when there is any trouble. I know it is said to be impossible to approach, let alone enter, but we must regain control of the First Warren! The Great Wood will follow."

"What about the prince?" came a shout from down in the crowd. "Prince Jupiter Smalls?"

"Let me finish, please." Bleston said. Heather noticed Tameth Seer, his face set in a smug sneer at the uneasy crowd. Bleston went on. "I have been determined—for years I've been determined—to return to the First Warren and assert my claim. But my brother's rule prospered. He ushered in a golden age of rabbit civilization. I kept up, by my own secret means, with what happened at court and with his many wars. My heart went out to him when he fell, and I wondered if it was time for me to return and reclaim my place. I wanted to bring the ethic of Terralain, that every rabbit can be a king, to all of Natalia. It took some years, and many things had to be set in order, but I set out from Terralain with this intent."

The unrest in the crowd swelled, and Heather saw Captain Frye's lieutenants gather around him, uncertain what to do. Picket stepped away from Bleston. Emma and Heather followed him.

"Friends," Bleston said, turning toward the three rabbits on stage. "Hear me out. Have I not earned this?"

Picket paused. "You have, Prince," he said. "But I beg you to consider what your words mean."

Bleston nodded, then pointed at Heather. "This young rabbit has spoken to me," he said. "And it is because of her, the Scribe of the Cause, that I have made a decision." Heather's heart pounded. Tameth Seer sneered, and the crowd quieted. "When Prince Jupiter Smalls returns," he said, raising the ruby high, "I will personally hang the Whitson Stone around his neck and pledge my allegiance to him as bearer of the Green Ember and Natalia's rightful heir. I will stand beside him and serve him all his days. United, we will fight Morbin Blackhawk and end the reign of terror under the Lords of Prey. We shall reclaim the First Warren and, at last, bring into being the Mended Wood!"

Chapter Twenty-Seven

REVELS ENDED

The crowd surged forward, cheering loud and long, awash in relief and exultant in joy. The room exploded with happy shouts.

"The Silver Prince!" they cried. "Long live the Legend of Terralain, the Savior of Halfwind! Hail the Silver Prince!"

They clamored around the stage, shouting his name, praising him more vigorously than on the day he saved them from the attack. Picket shook his hand and joined in the celebration. Heather crossed to hug him. She wept, feeling a swelling pride and surging hope in her heart.

She turned to Picket and hugged him long and hard. She hugged Emma too, and the three friends danced on stage as the vibrant celebratory music resumed. Loud as it was, it could hardly be heard over the raucous cheers that filled the room. Discordant songs broke out in honor of the Silver Prince and Prince Jupiter Smalls.

It was a wildly happy scene, and Heather let herself enjoy it. She danced, leapt, sang along, and hugged a hundred strangers. It was clear that she and Picket weren't the only ones who had been anxious about what Bleston's presence meant for the prince.

She saw Helmer standing at the back of the hall, a scowl on his face. But even his disobeying orders and leaving the hospital couldn't upset her on this night. She shook her head as he limped off, and she ran to hug another neck.

She watched Picket and Emma, hand in hand, dancing a jig beside the musicians. How far he had come since the days when Emma had called him "Shuffler" and he'd spent weeks moping around Cloud Mountain. Fresh tears came, and she ran to them, joining in their exuberant dance.

* * *

Picket hadn't been so happy in ages. He sang along with the raucous songs and danced like a fool for the joy swelling inside him. Captain Frye came by and clapped his back. He turned and hugged the old soldier, and they made an unspoken peace.

The appearance of the captain sent a stab of regret through Picket as he remembered his imprudent advice to Smalls. But surely, with the support of Bleston, the prince's cause had never been more favorable. Smalls would be king, and, supported by Bleston, he had a real chance to win.

"I wish the prince were here!" Emma shouted, trying to be heard above the noise.

"Me too," he agreed. "With any luck he'll be in Kingston by now. And if news reaches the conference that

Bleston has pledged his support, no lord of any citadel will stand in his way."

"It's amazing," Heather said. "I can't remember ever being this happy!"

"If only Morbin will not act too quickly," Captain Frye said, "and we can gather all the citadels under the prince's banner. We may have time to prepare an answer that evil old bird will remember."

They sang. They danced. They ate and drank. The night stretched on and the revels faded, leading at last to deep, peaceful sleep and a slow start in the morning.

* * *

Picket arrived early at the Fowlers' course and found Perkinson already there.

"My, but you're an early riser," Picket said. "Or a never-went-to-sleeper."

"I slept a little," he said. "But I don't need much sleep to outwork you."

"We'll see about that," Picket said, smiling.

"Aren't we supposed to work together?" Coleden asked, jogging up.

"Everything's a competition with those two," Jo Shanks said, joining them. "Even teamwork."

"And," Picket said, "you're last, Jo."

"We all know what that means," Perk said, smiling and rubbing his hands together.

"I don't know what it means," Cole said.

"Oh, right," Perk said. "New guy doesn't know what it means."

"Tell him what it means, Jo," Picket said.

"It means," he said with a scowl, "that I have to set up the obstacles." He trotted off, yawning as he went. "I thought you'd be different while Captain Helmer's out."

"You thought wrong," Picket said. "I follow in my master's footsteps."

"That's a little terrifying," Heather said, blocking her own yawn as she appeared on the course. "Are you really going to make Jo set up with his bad arm?"

"His poor arm!" Perk cried.

"Let's wrap it tight with love!" Cole said, smiling. They all laughed. All except Heather.

"That's fantastic, bucks," she said. "Real clever stuff. Just wait till it's your arm I'm treating. I might not be as gentle."

"We all know," Picket said, loud enough for Jo to hear, "that Jo's arm requires an intense level of tenderness."

She smirked at him, then laughed.

Picket winked at her. Then, over her head, he noticed two rabbits coming their way. Captain Frye and a limping Captain Helmer. "Something's up," he said. "Stay here and get things going, Perk." Perk nodded as Picket and Heather crossed to meet them.

Before Heather could ask why Captain Helmer was out of bed, she stopped, seeing the serious look on the two veterans' faces. Picket panicked, thinking of Smalls.

186

"Is it the prince?" he asked. Heather turned to look at her brother, confused.

"What do you mean? Is Smalls in danger?" she asked.

Helmer held up his hand. "It's Cloud Mountain," he said. "Morbin's army is moving on Cloud Mountain."

"Pacer just arrived with an urgent request for aid," Captain Frye added. "The Silver Prince is mustering the entire army on Westfield now. We had hoped for more time to unify the factions, but we won't have it."

"Pack your gear," Helmer called. "The Fowlers—all of us—are going to war."

Chapter Twenty-Eight

Bird Food

Heather prepared her satchel for the grisly work that lay ahead. She sighed, seeing Aunt Jone's patchy purse inside. She must speak to Bleston about releasing the old rabbit. But was there time? She shoved more vials and cloth on top of the crumbling purse, and in a few minutes she had forgotten about Jone in her hasty packing. She was distressed. This was war, and they were not prepared.

There would be no time to mass an army from every secret citadel. No time to join with the holdouts and the far-flung militias in a tenuous alliance. No time to form a force capable of winning a victory against Morbin's far-superior army. No. Morbin's strategy was brilliant. He was attacking the least defended area, the place with the fewest soldiers, where the most free civilians lived.

She wondered how much Garten Longtreader, her betraying uncle, had been involved with this plan. Until recently, Cloud Mountain had been a secret. Now it was facing attack, and she could only hope they weren't too late to help. She hoped other citadels would get word in time to come to their aid. Much as it plagued her, she couldn't fight the war alone. She was a field medic attached to the Fowlers. They were certain to be in the thick of the fighting.

She would see terrible things.

"Bring all the tonic you can," Emma said, packing several bags at once and passing them off to various assistants. "Help me pack first, please, Heather."

Heather obeyed, dropping her own work to join Emma. "Where will you be?" she asked.

"I'll be going ahead of the army to Cloud Mountain," she said. "I'm going to prep the main hall for casualties, along with Doctor Zeiger and the team there."

"And me?" Heather asked, a catch in her voice.

Emma stopped and looked her friend in the eyes. Her gaze was steady and her face set. Heather had no doubt of her friend's royal blood. She was King Jupiter's daughter, more composed than Heather thought possible. "Listen, Heather. I love you very much. You're my dearest friend. But you must be brave. To save lives, we will endure terrible things. We serve an army of rabbits who offer themselves freely for the cause." She touched Heather's shaking hand. "For them, we must do no less than our best."

Heather wanted to say that she was worried about more than the battle and the blood. She wanted to say how fearful she was for Emma's life. She wanted to unburden herself of the secret she carried. But she only nodded. "I am with you, my sister."

Emma nodded gravely, then threw herself back into the work.

* * *

Picket couldn't believe how long it took to muster the army. He had been in battle before, but he had yet to move with a force this large in a planned action. It was excruciatingly slow. The Fowlers packed, prepped, and waited on Westfield for hours while supplies were moved and other divisions made their preparations. The catapults had been moved ahead of the army, and Heyward was part of the team of brother votaries overseeing their delivery. Picket hoped they would arrive in time at the place Bleston had chosen, along with their accompanying wagons of ammunition. He paced back and forth, muttering as the hours dragged.

"You have to relax, Picket," Heather said, coming beside him and whispering in his ear. "The other Fowlers are looking to you."

He glanced at the others. They *were* looking at him. "They all have more experience than I do, anyway."

"That doesn't matter," she said. "You're a leader. You lead by what you do and by what you don't do."

He frowned. "You're right," he said. Then he addressed the Fowlers, who were pacing and fidgeting. "Let's all take it easy and try to rest. I know there's no real sleeping now, but let's lie down for a bit."

Coleden nodded and went to his pack. Unrolling his blanket, he lay down and closed his eyes. The others smirked, but they imitated him, and soon all but Heather and Picket were laid out and resting.

"War is a splash of terror in a sea of boredom," Heather said, "At least that's what Helmer says."

"He ought to know," Picket replied. "I'm worried about Emma. She's going ahead, into who knows what kind of danger, and there's only a small team with her."

"I know," she agreed. "I tried to intervene, but she's my superior. And I couldn't get to Captain Frye in time. She was already gone."

"I'm sorry."

"Heyna Blackstar went with her," Heather added. "That's some comfort. The poor doe is still not well, but there was nothing Emma could do to stop her. She was positively immovable."

"Good girl," Picket said.

"Agreed."

"I wish Smalls were here."

"I do too," she said. "Though, if today goes badly, it may be better if he isn't."

"If it goes badly, Heather, I think Smalls' cause is doomed anyway. Losing this battle means losing all. I don't think we could recover."

"Uncle Wilfred would know," she said. "I wish he were here. I wish any of our family were here."

"One day, we'll all be together again," he said, a wan

smile on his face. "But not yet. Before that day, this." He gestured toward the massing apparatus of war, the streaming soldiers and the banks of archers. Supply wagons disappeared on the trail, moving away from Halfwind as Westfield teemed with warriors under a sky broken by banners.

They stood together, Heather slipping her arm inside her brother's. She rested her head on his shoulder and gazed at the simmering brew of battle.

The Silver Prince appeared with Captains Frye and Valter and a still-limping Helmer. Lieutenant Kout, Tameth Seer, and the other leaders were huddling around a hastily erected platform. Picket noticed that Bleston's shirt bore a new symbol. It was really a combination of several old symbols, a shield divided into three parts. On one showed the black field and silver stars of Terralain. On another, the blood moon and crossed spears of Halfwind were displayed. The third, and largest, showed the double-diamond symbol, one red and one green side by side. Flag-bearers carried their banners to the prince, and all these symbols were present. Highest of all, and borne by a stout rabbit, was a huge flag marked with the double-diamond emblem. Picket thought of Smalls, who would inherit the consequences of this day, for good or ill.

Lieutenant Kout stepped forward and raised his arms for silence. "Today the Silver Prince will lead us into battle!" A brief cheer erupted, but Kout raised his arms again, waving the crowd to silence. "Please, we must get on. King

Bleston will address as many as can hear, but he asks that all the captains and lieutenants move to the front, so they can be clear on the battle plan."

Picket looked at Perkinson and Heather. "That's you, Pick," Perkinson said. "Go on, Lieutenant. I can take care of these baby bucks. I think Cole is actually asleep."

"I'm awake," Cole said from the ground, without moving or opening his eyes.

"And Jo," Perk said, "is probably over there dreaming about getting his poor little arm wrapped."

Jo, who hadn't been sleeping but was still lying down, shot up and threw off his blanket. "I am not!"

Picket shook his head and moved toward the platform. Before he could reach the front, a young soldier stopped him.

"Lord Picket," the soldier said. "I'm so honored to see you meet—to, um—meet you," he stammered, offering his hand.

Picket smiled and shook it. "I'm not a lord. I'm just a soldier. What's your name?"

"I'm nobody, sir," he said. "I mean, I'm just infantry. I'm bird food."

"I asked for your name, soldier."

"Lallo, sir."

"Where are you from?"

"Sir, I was from the Great Wood—back before. I lived along the lakeshore. We could see the islands from our house. Forbidden Island used to give me nightmares."

Picket smiled. "How long have you been at Halfwind?"

"A few years, sir. I like it here, but it's no Citadel of Dreams." He laughed and a few of his companions nodded.

"I've never been to the Great Wood, Lallo," Picket said.

"It was a good place once, my mother said. But the afterterrors…well, it's not so great now."

"Your father?"

"Lost," he said, "before I was old enough to remember."

"I hear you," Picket said, placing a hand on Lallo's shoulder. "Listen, tomorrow you'll take back, with interest, what's been taken from you. You're bird food? I'm bird food. I'm infantry too. I'm stuck right in there with you. We're too stupid to know we don't have a chance."

More and more of Lallo's fellows were gathering around. They were ordinary soldiers. Scared. Excited. "The infantry carries the day, bucks, or the day won't be carried." Picket glanced up and saw that Bleston was motioning for silence. "I've got to go, bucks. Be bold out there. I'll see you on the battlefield." They clapped him on the back as he made his way forward.

Chapter Twenty-Nine

A BLAST OF WOE

Today," Bleston called. "Today we march to war. If all goes well, tomorrow's dawn will be a red one. I have no great speech for you, friends. This only will I say: Tomorrow is a day of turns. Tomorrow is the day we make Morbin quake on his stolen throne. Tomorrow we turn the tide for Jupiter's son!"

As the army cheered, Picket saw Kyle—Kylen—limping with a determined grimace onto the stage. Bleston glanced over, and his face betrayed a moment of surprise, and anguish, before his poise returned. He faced the crowd. "My son, Prince Kylen, has come to see us off. I have asked him to stay behind and lead this citadel in my absence."

Some clapped, some called support, while a murmur grew among the crowd.

Kylen walked forward, raising his arms as his father had done. Into the new silence, he spoke. "Actually, Father, I'm happy to say that I will be joining you on the march and in the battle. If your blood is spilled," he shouted hoarsely to the crowd, "my blood is spilled!" Before they could respond with their enthusiastic cheers, he drew and raised his sword, placing his other hand over his heart. "My place beside you," he shouted, and the army joined in, "my blood for yours! Till the Green Ember rises, or the end of the world!"

To Picket, who shouted along with the whole host of rabbits, it felt more like the beginning of the world.

After the crowd quieted again, the Silver Prince laid out his plan. Kylen stood, though it was noticeably difficult for him. Picket listened, feeling an optimism he had never yet felt as a soldier. For now, the battle dread was quiet within him. He had the sense that anything was possible, and he was filled with hopeful expectation.

We might do something amazing today.

Then came a quick, dull sound of a blast in the distance. Bleston froze, then turned to his council.

"It's a signal from the far perimeter," Captain Frye said. "One blast means a moderate warning, perhaps urgent news or a lone wolf spotted. Two would mean," he paused to listen, "a far more serious situation."

There was no second blast, and Bleston turned to Frye. "A small team?"

"Yes," Frye agreed. He scanned the crowd.

"Sir," Picket called, "the Fowlers can check it out."

"Very well," Bleston said. "Meet us on the road." Then, calling above the murmuring crowd, Bleston cried, "We move out!"

The officers found their charges, and the great force,

with all its varied units, began the march toward Cloud Mountain.

Picket found his unit ready. "This way," he called, and they followed him through the moving army, on a divergent but nearly parallel course into the forest.

"Pick," Cole said, jogging up beside him. "I'm new here, but I'm pretty sure the way to Cloud Mountain is, well, the way the rest of the army is going."

"Very astute, Cole," Picket said. "Let's pick up the pace. We need to check out the source of that sentinel warning." Cole nodded, and they hurried on.

* * *

Heather ran alongside the rest of the Fowlers, her satchel slapping rhythmically with each stride. Snow began to fall, soft and slowly, settling on the trees. In a few minutes they reached the sentinel station. She saw the grey twist of smoke still rising through the trees but could see no sign of the guards. It was quiet. Far too quiet.

She heard a stirring in the thick knot of pines ahead. Picket reached for his sword, drawing it slowly. Perk and Cole followed his lead, drawing swords. But Jo, hovering at Picket's elbow, nocked two arrows and peered into the trees.

They heard a noise like a muffled growl from the woods, though Heather could make no sense of it. She saw a hint of grey fur, and something lurched out of the forest.

Heather screamed.

It was Uncle Wilfred, and he was badly wounded. He stumbled for a few steps, then fell sprawling onto the cold ground.

Heather dashed ahead of the others. She found her uncle facedown, not moving. She rolled him over and gasped, then dug in her satchel and went to work. Setting aside Aunt Jone's tattered purse, she found the tonic, bandages, and ointment she needed.

Picket gently lifted Uncle Wilfred's head while Heather forced him to drink a little of Emma's tonic. "Is he going to—" Picket began.

"Not if I can help it."

After a minute, Uncle Wilfred coughed and moaned. His eyes flashed open.

"Hang on," Heather said, still tending his wounds as best she could. "We're here, Uncle Wilfred. We'll take care of you."

"Oh," he moaned. "My dear ones," he began, but he fell into a coughing fit. When he had recovered enough to speak, he looked sadly at Heather and Picket. Tears filled his eyes and spilled onto the grey fur of his face.

"Uncle?"

"Where's Emma?"

"She's on her way to Cloud Mountain, ahead of the army," Picket said. "Morbin is attacking."

Uncle Wilfred's eyes widened. He tried to stand, but another fit of coughing overtook him.

"Please, Uncle," Heather said, soothing him. He lay

down, propped against Picket's arms. "Don't try to move. Don't talk."

"I have to…" he said. "We must…must secure the princess…we must…"

"Uncle, what's happened?" Heather said.

"My dear," Uncle Wilfred said, as the tears flowed. "I'm sorry…so sorry to have to—"

"No," Heather said.

"No," Picket said. "No, no, no…"

He looked from Picket to Heather, his face a picture of anguish. He grabbed Heather's hands.

"Smalls…is dead."

Chapter Thirty

HOPELESS GOING

Heather reeled. She fell back, blinking, unbelieving. She felt as though she'd been struck in the head with the flat of a fat sword. She clenched at her neck, desperately clutching her necklace. No sound could penetrate her ears, no thought could enter her mind. And the silence went on and on.

It was broken by the sound of a wild, woeful scream. Her own scream. The pain was unbearable. She dropped to her knees, tears coming in a rush. She felt someone come beside her, wrap her in an embrace. That someone—she couldn't say who it was—held her as she rocked.

"We have to help him." She knew the voice. It was a voice from long ago. It came to her from far away, as far as Nick Hollow. Blinking through her tears, she saw it was Picket, her little brother. And he was right in front of her. "Heather, we need you. Uncle Wilfred is bad off."

Of course. The sounds of the woods came back to her. She was aware of the others, of the limp form on the ground. She could not, not in this moment, indulge her pain any longer. She shook her head, dashed the tears from her eyes, and crossed back to her uncle. His eyes were closed. She felt his pulse. *Weak, but still alive.* "We need to get him to the hospital. Back to Halfwind."

"What about Emma?" Picket said, his face contorted. "We have to do something. She's the heir now. We have to find her, protect her."

"We're marching to war, Pick," she said. "Where can she go that's safer than Cloud Mountain?"

"But if we lose—" he began.

"If we lose," she said, touching his arm, "then all is lost anyway. You said it yourself."

"But we can't just leave her alone."

"Of course," she said. She rubbed her face with her hands and stood. "Why don't I go ahead to Cloud Mountain as fast as I can, and you take Uncle Wilfred back to Halfwind? Then we—I don't know—we proceed with the plan? You do your part in the battle and I do mine. And I'll look after Emma as best I can."

"I'll go with her." Perkinson stepped forward. He nodded to Picket. "I'll accompany Heather, grabbing some other bucks I trust as we pass the army on the way. We'll go ahead to Cloud Mountain, and I'll keep watch over them, Picket. You, Cole, and Jo can get Captain Wilfred to the hospital and see that he's looked after. Then you can catch up to the army, and," he laid his hand on Picket's shoulder, "I'll see you on the field."

Picket glanced at Uncle Wilfred, frowned, then looked

to Heather. She nodded. "Okay, Perk. But please, my friend, take care of them."

"My place beside you, brother," he said, embracing Picket.

Heather gave Picket detailed instructions. Then she draped on her satchel, kissed her uncle gently on the forehead, rose, and wrapped Picket in a long embrace. She felt his tears on her neck. She squeezed him tight.

Then, without saying another word, she broke the embrace and turned, hurrying away.

Perkinson ran to catch up with her, and she heard the sounds of the others slowly lifting Uncle Wilfred.

"I'm so sorry," Perkinson said, as he caught up. "It's an awful thing to lose a friend."

She turned on him, anger flashing in her eyes. "A friend?" she said. "A friend? I have not just lost a friend, Perkinson. *We* have lost—the whole world has lost!—a great and noble rabbit. We have lost our hope. The Green Ember is snuffed out, and the new world will never flourish now as it should have. Smalls is dead. Hope is dead."

Chapter Thirty-One

MANY WOUNDS

Picket's insides felt like sawdust and ashes. He fought a private battle within himself against a foe more terrible than any bird. Somehow, he carried on, holding back the grief, the surging guilt.

It took him and his companions several hours to get Uncle Wilfred properly situated back at Halfwind, and Picket was reluctant to leave him. He was still very bad off, and the nurse would not say if he would recover. Yet Uncle Wilfred seemed to be regaining a little focus after drinking the tonic Heather prescribed.

"Picket," he said, his eyes fluttering open. "Picket, my lad. Thank you. Thank you." He smiled for a moment, then his face contorted as memory seemed to return. "Oh, no," he said, tears starting in his eyes again. "Oh, no."

"Uncle," Picket said, leaning over him and clasping his hand, "what happened?"

This was the question Picket had been terrified to ask. But he had to know.

"Folly, lad," Uncle Wilfred said. He took an offered

drink from a hovering nurse and went on. "Defying every wise advisor, Smalls was determined to go to the mining camp and liberate the slaves," he said. "The camp was crawling with birds. Most of our team was carried off. The slaves, and I assume your father, all killed or carried off. All was chaos and woe. Smalls fought like Whitson himself, like his father, as heroic as ever I've seen a rabbit fight. But in the end, there were too many birds. He was run through and… carried off…limp as a string."

Picket felt the words enter his ears and race like poison to his heart. He dropped Uncle Wilfred's hand, suddenly afraid that by his touch he might infect his uncle, hastening his death. He felt like his hands were dirty, his presence toxic, that he had to get away from these rabbits before he ruined them all.

"What have I done?" he whispered, wiping his hands on his shirt. "It's my fault. I've killed him."

"No, no, son," Uncle Wilfred said, wincing. "How can you say that? You weren't there. I was there. I saw it all, and I could do nothing. It's my fault, Picket, not yours."

"Uncle, you tried to stop him doing it, and I'm certain you did all you could to save him," Picket said, "but I begged him to do it."

"You…you begged him to attack the camp?" Uncle Wilfred said, disbelieving. "You can't have, Picket. You didn't know. There's no way—"

"I knew," Picket said, shouting at the ceiling. "I knew! Smalls told me about the camp and he told me you all advised against it and," he dug at his eyes, "I asked him to try anyway! I told him Heather would be devastated if she found out he hadn't, which probably wasn't even true. But I wanted them free. I wanted to see my father again. I wanted to save my mother, to keep my word to little Jacks. I made Smalls do it, and his death is on me. It's my fault."

Looking up, Picket saw that Uncle Wilfred's face had frozen in a mask of grief. Glancing across at Cole and Jo, he read their astonished disapproval. Though they quickly looked away, he saw it. And in an awful way he savored it. He knew he deserved it. Uncle Wilfred sank back on his bed, his eyes closed and his face still set with pain.

Picket took it all in, the misery and guilt, rolling it around in his mouth like a fine wine. He stood, turning away from his uncle. Neither Jo nor Cole would meet his gaze. He had to leave, had to get as far from this place as he could. He walked to the door.

"Stop him!" Uncle Wilfred shouted as Picket made to dash out. Cole rushed to block the door, and Jo grabbed him from behind. Picket struggled intensely for a few moments, then finally relented. "Come back, Picket," his uncle said, his words heavy with hurt, his voice cracking in his pain and weakness.

Picket let himself be led to his uncle's bedside. He sat heavily on the chair beside the bed. His heart felt shredded to bits.

"I have lived with this same woe, my lad," Uncle Wilfred said, placing his hand gently on Picket's bowed head. "I was too slow to realize my brother's treachery, and so Garten got to the old king, and Morbin committed his foulest crime. And I saw it, saw the result of my folly. Now I've seen the result of yours. Yes, yes," he said, patting Picket's head, "I agree that you were wrong. I see that your advice was bad and that you have some stock in the blame. But do not take it all. A prince will hear bad advice, and he must make his own choices."

"But I put an unfair burden on him," Picket said weakly. "I'm ashamed to say it, but I…I manipulated him."

"Yes, that was wrong. And now the prince is gone. You should own this mistake, but you must not take credit for the enemy's work. You didn't capture innocent rabbits and hold them captive to work your mines. You didn't murder Smalls' father and leave him abandoned with an unimaginable burden. You didn't leave him to die at Jupiter's Crossing all those months ago. No, son. You are on the right side of this war. You were only on the wrong side of this advice. And the prince, this rabbit who was wise and bold, erred in taking it."

"I can't just forget this, Uncle."

"You don't have to, Picket. You should own your part. But you'll have to do it quickly. Own it, and move forward. Today, a host of rabbits moves to fight the battle for which Smalls lived and died. Today, his enemies mass near a mountain where the princess, unaware of who she is, works in danger. You cannot spend weeks in self-indulgent misery as you once did. You cannot give in to your grief. You must carry on and bear the flame."

"I don't know if I can."

"You must. To bear the flame means more than only holding on to the fire kindled in the Green Ember's rising. It means to bear the fatal flames of the enemy, to bear up under the scorching heat of these hateful days."

"I can't bear it."

"There is no other way, Picket. Would you stay here with the aged, with the mothers and their children? Would you lie in bed with the lame and sick while your brothers fight in the field, while Heather and Emma work in Morbin's shadow?"

"Of course not," he said, anger flashing in his eyes.

"Then rouse yourself, lad," Uncle Wilfred growled. "Many wounds will bloom in this battle, and you will carry yours inside you. But carry them and fight on. Fight for Smalls, for Emma, for Heather and the whole wounded world. Carry your pain and let it fire you in the fight. Bear the burden and bear the flame."

Picket nodded and blinked back tears. "I will go, Uncle."

"Fight for me, Picket," Wilfred said, his cough returning. The nurse, eyes worried, coughed quietly. Cole came to stand beside Picket.

"We have to go, Pick," he said.

Picket nodded. "I love you, Uncle. I will try to make you proud."

"You already have, son," he said. "You and Heather must be for Emma what I have been for Smalls. I lay that charge on you, son, though I know it's heavy. You and Heather must save Emma, preserve the princess for the Mended Wood. I so badly wish I could come. I know the odds are bad."

"We may have a chance," Picket said, "with Bleston on our side."

Uncle Wilfred's eyes widened, and his hand closed around Picket's, squeezing tightly. That motion was the last sign of his strength. He sank back. The nurse rushed to his side and examined him. Picket stepped away, frightened.

"He needs rest," the nurse said. "He's had a terrible ordeal. I'm afraid you'll have to go," she said. "Please!"

"Will he be okay?" Picket asked, backing toward the door.

"I don't know," she said.

* * *

Many hours later, as the sun touched the tops of the far mountains and bathed the sky in purple and peach, Picket, Cole, and Jo made the last turn in the road and saw the sprawling war camp. This was only half the army, as it had divided according to Bleston's scheme. Picket had thought of going straight to Cloud Mountain, to be at Emma's side. But he needed to tell Captains Frye and Helmer about what had happened to the prince. And he had made a promise that morning to a young soldier named Lallo, to fight with him on the field. Besides, he wanted, needed, to fight. This was Picket's part, to join Captains Frye and Helmer and the bulk of the Halfwind force, to help lead the Fowlers into war.

Picket scanned the camp and saw soldiers huddled around fires, talking softly and preparing to bed down. They were settling, hoping to find some rest in the shadow before the blaze of battle that awaited them at dawn.

Picket saw Heyward, blue robe swishing as he bent over a mess of metal fittings and wooden rods, whittling on the ends of the rods with his knife. He moved to lock down a connection, then reached for a bolt of black cloth. He unrolled it and squinted, frowning at the components before him with a cocked head. After counting out something on his fingers, he drew out his shears and went to work on the thick fabric.

Picket smiled at his friend, though Heyward couldn't see him. Always tinkering. Picket wanted to go to him, to talk to his old friend by the fire while he worked away at sunset. But he had more urgent business.

Picket found Frye and Helmer at the central fire, going over the war plan with their lieutenants.

"Lieutenant Longtreader," Captain Frye said. "I was beginning to wonder if you planned on missing the battle altogether."

"I'm sorry, sir," Picket said. "I was delayed by—" He was unsure how to proceed.

Helmer caught Picket's eye, recognized his baneful look. "Thank you, lieutenants," he said to the gathered officers. "I think you all know the plan well enough by now. Try to get some sleep, bucks. Dawn will break on us, and then—well, then we will break on our enemy."

"Yes, sir!" the officers said. They gathered their things and, nodding to Picket, left.

"Sit, Picket," Captain Frye said. "You're exhausted, son."

Picket sat, his head down.

"What's happened?" Helmer asked, grave and attentive.

"The worst," Picket said.

"Prince Smalls?" Frye asked.

Picket nodded.

Chapter Thirty-Two

CLANGS AND WHISPERS

Heather and Perkinson, accompanied by five stout soldiers, entered through the misty mouth of Cloud Mountain's hidden cave. Heather hadn't been here in months, and she longed for the welcoming aromas of the Savory Den. But when she entered the large room, there was no one there. It was dark and silent, with not a solitary torch to see by. She remembered good meals among friends, laughter and love, and hard moments as well. She thought of how Chef Gort always seemed to hang around until someone complimented his food. She remembered the day Kyle had stood up to Captain Frye. So much had happened since then.

The guards in green led them on, through the secret wall, down the passage and to the stairs.

"We know our way from here," Perkinson said, nodding to the Forest Guards. He thanked the accompanying soldiers and told them they could report to the Cloud Mountain officers to be reassigned for the battle. They bowed and left, accompanied by the guards in green.

"Have you been here before?" Heather asked.

"Yes, a few times."

"I'm going to find Emma," she said.

"Of course." They'd been surrounded by soldiers for most of the journey, so they hadn't spoken about Emma's true identity.

"You will keep Emma's secret?" she asked.

"I will," he said.

"What will you do?"

"I'll make myself useful, Heather. I want to get back down to the valley, but I may only make it to King Bleston's forces on the mountainside."

Heather frowned and turned for the steps. "I have to go. Thanks for coming with me, Perk. If you see Picket on the field, please look out for him."

"I'll do my part," he said. "Take care of yourself, Heather. This battle will shake many things loose. I hope you're flexible enough to adapt."

She started up the steps, then turned. "What do you mean?"

But Perkinson was gone.

She frowned, then bounded up the stairs three at a time. Reaching the top, she was surprised to see King's Garden undisturbed. Glancing briefly at Lighthall, she hurried along the path, past the statues of King Whitson and Captain Blackstar, and down the long passage to Hallway Round.

Passing through the open door, she heard the humming noise of rabbits in motion. At the end of the passage, she entered the large stone hallway. Rabbits were bustling in and out of the two large doors to her left, while anxious guards stood watch over the barrels of blastpowder. There used to be only one. Now five wooden barrels, bound with hoops of brass, stood stacked and ready to be blown in the event of an invasion.

She was staring at the commotion, spotting here and there a familiar face, when rabbits began to notice her. They bowed, waved, and hurried on their way. Some pointed and whispered, eyes suddenly alight. But none stopped. Everyone had a task, and the community was churning with purpose.

"Where's Doctor Zeiger?" she asked one of the guards.

"Hello, Miss Longtreader," he said, bowing. "The doctors are setting up in the great hall."

"Thank you." She moved on, lingering for a moment beside the door to the foggy porch. Would she find Mrs. Weaver out there? She wasn't sure, but she didn't have time now. She opened the door to the great hall and walked inside.

The hall had been altered. The stalls and shops, the makeshift market, all were replaced by a functioning factory of war. The doctors and nurses made use of a large portion of the hall, prepping their cures and staging their stations and patients' bedding. In the alcoves along the walls, fletchers made arrows and coopers prepped barrels, and the smithy rang with the clang and shatter of hammered steel as swords and other weapons were forged. Sparks splashed around a dozen rabbits in black as they beat at blades or pumped the bellows. Heather hurried to the hospital area and, seeing a familiar face, smiled.

"Hello, Doctor Zeiger," she said.

"Miss Longtreaders! To be sure it's you being yourself and not any somebody other," Doctor Zeiger said. "Coming to help, you is? We's needing every hand we can take, but I thinked you were battlefield medic for Crazy Helmer's big fancy Fowler squad?"

"I got, um, reassigned here," she said. "I need to find Emma."

"Oh, Doctor Emma's being very help to mine as we preparate good job for bad job of war."

"It looks like you're doing all you can, Doc," she said, frowning at the loud clatter from the smithy.

"It's big medicine this music we get for our hospital, yes?"

"It's awful."

"Mine think hammer heads might stop after we get first batch of wound-hurt rabbits here, but Lord Rake say that army still have to weapon make and weapon fix, so we get big-time happy clitter-clatter-bang-brack all days, all nights."

"I hope you get some relief," she said. "Please excuse, me, Doc. I have to find Emma."

He pointed to the station where Emma stood, directing some other doctors in how to prepare the tonic. One took notes while she mixed ingredients from a table full of jars.

Another listened intently while crushing something green with a pestle. Heather saw Heyna Blackstar among those hovering near Emma, her scarred face alert and actively scanning the hall. Doctor Zeiger went on. "She is make good medicine, our Emma. Better her work is than hundred new clingy-clang swords."

"There was always more to her than any of us knew," she said. Smiling at Doctor Zeiger, she turned and walked toward Emma.

"What are you doing here?" Emma called. "Is something wrong?"

Heather nodded, tears starting in her eyes.

Emma stepped closer, taking Heather's hands in her own. "What is it? Is Picket all right?"

"Yes," she said, wiping at her eyes. "He's fine. Can we go somewhere a bit quieter to talk?"

"Yes, dear. I just have to finish this list of ingredients. We have a lot of tonic to produce. We're nearly done. Meet me…" She frowned, looking around for a quiet corner.

"Where's Lord Rake?" Heather asked.

"I think he's up behind the village and the caves, where the old votary camp was. He's with his captains, preparing for the battle. He's been scheming about how to defend this place for years. It looks like he'll finally get a chance to test his plans."

"I hope they work," Heather said. "So much depends on it. I'll be there, Emma dear."

"I'll see you up there in a bit," Emma said. Shaken, she returned to her work.

Heather nodded and walked off. As she did, she heard whispers all around her. She noticed now that rabbits here had recognized her and that her presence had created a small stir in the hall. She thought of Emma. If only they all knew who had been with them already—who had been with them for years and years—and how special she was.

Heather tried to ignore the whispers, but she couldn't help hearing those close by as they raised their voices above the rattling din of the smithy.

"It's her! The Scribe of the Cause."

"That's Heather Longtreader, the reason we say 'bear the flame.'"

"She's the poetess of the Mended Wood."

"She's an inspiration to us all. I'm glad she's here. It's bound to bring the prince's cause good fortune."

"I spoke to her once. She was very kind, showed interest in me and everything. A real nice rabbit."

"They say she'll be our queen one day."

"I've heard that rumor too. I hope ever so much that it's true."

Heather left the great hall with its shattering clatter, its whispering rabbits, and its many medical preparations, wounded in a way no tonic could cure.

Chapter Thirty-Three

THE END OF THE WORLD

Heather rushed out into the open air atop Cloud Mountain. The village green was browning, and the gardens had been harvested many weeks before. She walked on, past stone tables and through still-neat hedgerows. She glanced at Helmer's scarred maple and marveled at the toddling buck playing beneath it. As she watched, the little rabbit's mother came along to scold him and snatch him up. Where had all the other younglings gone? She guessed they were somewhere inside the mountain, secreted away with wary protectors while the rest made their grim preparations for war.

A cart piled with small barrels was being pulled by twelve strong rabbits, and a squad of thirty tall archers marched in good order toward the caves ahead. She nodded to a soldier hurrying past and said hello to a contemplative votary who walked the edges of the village, whispering invocations.

"Where is the way to the standing stones, brother?" she asked.

"Ah, they are easy to find, Miss. Though I'm very sorry to say that they are overrun by the machines of war."

"Which way?"

He pointed to the cave where the last archer disappeared. "If you follow them, Miss, you'll find your way."

"Thank you."

He touched his ears, his eyes, his mouth. "May you hear peace, see peace, and speak peace."

Heather nodded and jogged after the archers.

While she lived at Cloud Mountain, she had never been past the village to the caves beyond or the hermit's field on the other side of the caves. There had been a small collection of votaries living there, but no one bothered them, and few had been interested in the standing stones they haunted. Since the victory at Jupiter's Crossing and the revelation of the prince's cause in her story, however, devotion to the old ways had seen a resurgence.

Ducking into the narrow cave mouth, she made her way quickly along the passage. Sparse torches lit the long and winding tunnel, and as it stretched on and on, she began to run. The path bent steadily down. This part of Cloud Mountain must be on the edge, far lower down than the misty top where she had spent so much time. There were several junctions in the tunnel, leading she knew not where, but she stayed in the main passage.

The archers were nowhere to be seen. She began to worry she would never emerge, that she would spend the entire battle roaming the caves. But she soon saw a distant prick of light. She ran faster, and the light grew. At last she came to the end of the passage, and, squinting, she emerged from the cave onto a large plateau.

It was perhaps half the size of the village green above, and it teemed with active rabbits, all busy with preparations. As the sun sank to the edge of the mountains, she saw the standing stones in striking silhouettes before a peach and purple sky. But how were there so many? There were supposed to be seven, but she counted no less than fifteen. And some were oddly shaped.

As she moved closer, she realized that the edge of the plateau held more than the standing stones. It was lined with eight tall catapults.

The fog was thinner this low on the mountain. It glided past in silvery wisps, first obscuring the view and then blowing away on the wind. Several of the towering weapons were complete, but brothers in blue alongside green-clad soldiers worked to complete the last of them.

She gazed at one. Strong rabbits twisted long ropes tight inside the machine's complex innards. Heather was no engineer, but she imagined that the force they mustered was incredible. She couldn't believe that the machines, while sturdily built, could withstand the pressure. But she saw iron reinforcements along the wooden contraptions. *I hope they hold together.*

Everywhere barrels were stacked in heaps and officers shouted instructions to careful handlers. The archers she had followed emerged from the caves at a different point a hundred yards away. They trotted over to join a band of their comrades. There they separated into groups, all hard at work staging what looked to her like a thousand arrows.

Heather walked past the seven standing stones, awed by their careful crafting. These were taller than the ones at Halfwind and, unlike those in the Leaper's Hall, had winding stone stairs cut all around each stone. Each one could be climbed by a votary at rites or a pious rabbit seeking quiet contemplation. But she had no time for anything like that. She looked ahead.

Lord Rake was huddled with Pacer and several captains at a table between the archers and the catapults. He looked up and saw Heather, and his eyes narrowed. He motioned her over.

He finished a brief conference, dismissed his attendants, and asked her to sit. "What's happened, Heather?"

"Smalls," she began, but she could only hang her head, as no further words would come.

"He is lost?"

"Dead," she said in a ghostly whisper. "Uncle Wilfred has confirmed it."

"Wilfred saw the prince fall?" Lord Rake asked.

"Yes."

"Then it's certain." His head fell to his hands. "And we must assume there has been no conference at Kingston," he said, rising to pace, "no new coalition formed. No reinforcements coming."

"What does it mean?" she asked.

He pointed to the edge of the plateau, where a short, sturdy wall with a flat top lined the mountain's rim. "See for yourself."

She turned, walking past the last in a long row of catapults to the precipice's edge. A willowy sheet of fog was carried off as she sprang to the top of the wall and gazed into the distance.

She nearly fell, finding her balance only at the last moment.

An army filled the valley and the hills beyond. The ground was covered in wolves, clad in black and divided into regiments, banners flying and fires burning. The trees were covered with birds of prey, armored and armed with slashing blades and a chilling assortment of other weapons. The army was divided by a wide gap, with only a hint of the second force in sight. Reinforcements? She couldn't tell. She only knew that this was a scene that spoke clearly of the end of all things. It was the brooding womb of doom.

She stared for a long moment. "It really is the end of the world," she whispered. Lord Rake didn't answer. "We will all be lost," she said. "We'll all follow Smalls into death. It doesn't matter what we do. We can't stand against that! We have to get Emma out of here, give her a chance to survive and somehow, someday, rebuild what we lose in this battle."

Heather turned at last. Emma was there, standing beside Lord Rake, tears in her eyes. She had heard. She knew.

"I'll never abandon this community," Emma said, "no matter how many attack us."

"You're our leader now, my dear Emma," Lord Rake said, his face full of sorrow as he took her hands in his own. "You are Prince Smalls' sister and now Jupiter's heir. By rights, the Green Ember is yours now, though no one knows where it is."

"You will be our queen," Heather said, kneeling. "We have to get you to safety."

"Heather's right," Lord Rake said.

Emma shook her head, turned away, and took several long strides toward the caves. Heather thought she might run. Emma's body jerked with sobs. Then she settled onto her knees. Heather began to stand, but Lord Rake raised a hand. Emma needed time to think. Days. Weeks. But she had no time, and they all knew it.

Heather's mind was running through plans, working out ways to get Emma away in secret, as far from this certain doom as possible. After a moment, Emma turned to face them, then crossed to stand before them.

"Am I the heir?" she asked. Lord Rake nodded. "And I stand now in the place of…my brother, as leader of this alliance?"

"Yes, Princess Emma," he said. "You are in command."

She took a deep breath, swallowed hard, and released the breath slowly. "Then I command the following," she said, her voice trembling. "Everything must be as it was before. I have duties in the hospital, where I may save some lives by my efforts."

"You are Jupiter's heir, my dear. Your father would

want you—" Lord Rake began.

"Smalls was not," Emma interrupted. "That is, my brother was not here, and yet the battle plan was made. And you are the only father I have ever known," she said, looking into Lord Rake's eyes. "I trust you to proceed with the battle. I will be in the hospital treating the wounded, healing the hurt, seeing to the dead. If we survive tomorrow, then we can talk about what it means for me to be a princess. For now, my order is that everything must proceed as planned."

"Your Highness," Lord Rake said, bowing on one knee. "I will obey."

"And I," Heather said, remaining on her knees, "will always be faithful."

Chapter Thirty-Four

A DEFIANT CRY

Sween bore a large tray loaded with stinking glasses of wine. The glasses were long and lean, blown in the kilns of Akolan by master Milton Blenko. She was among fifteen slaves bringing wine, and they walked into Morbin's lair in five lines of three. Melody, the young rabbit not yet resigned to her slavery, walked behind her. Sween hated being in the room when the councils met. Though she would listen and report everything she heard when she returned to her quarters at Akolan, she knew it did little good. What was the point of collecting information that could never be used?

Perhaps it made them feel as if they weren't powerless. Mr. Weaver said her position so close to Morbin was no accident and that good would come of it in the end. It was what her husband had always said. Mr. Weaver had listened to her sing, and they talked for hours. She felt hopeful in a way she hadn't before her visit with the old rabbit, and the song inside her had come alive again. She was afraid she might absentmindedly begin singing at her work.

But that could not happen today. It must not. She focused on her task as they entered the chamber, striding in among the active conversation.

Morbin rested on his awful throne. General Flox, the white wolf who so terrified her, stood nearby with his stout lieutenant, Blenk. Five more Lords of Prey, including the ones she knew as Gern, Shelt, and Vardon, were gathered around.

And *him*. A grey rabbit.

"All is settled, Lord Morbin," the grey rabbit said, with an exaggerated bow.

He had his own cadre of rabbit officers, their uniforms like his, though lacking his proud flair. The room quieted.

"Good," Morbin said. "Is everything else in place?"

"It is," the rabbit said.

She had seen him in this place before, but she had always been able to get away from him. Now, thanks to Gritch's carefully orchestrated approach of the servers, she was forced to bow her head and raise her platter to him. He waited, not taking a glass. She held out for as long as possible, slowing the line so that Melody, directly behind her, began to groan with impatience. The last thing she wanted was for her, or Melody, to be noticed in this group. An anonymous slave was a living slave.

She had to look up at him, someone she despised as much, or more, than Morbin himself. He smiled at her, eyes proud as ever. But she thought she caught a hint of sadness. Was that regret, for what he had hoped would be their story? Or was it shame, for what he had done, what he was doing? She could not say.

He took the glass and she hurried on, serving each of the other rabbits in turn and then the wolves, while Melody followed behind.

"Lord Morbin, why not just crush them all now—eradicate them?" General Flox asked.

"Wolves are always hungry for an end to rabbitkind," Shelt, a brown falcon, said. "But for years we have had an arrangement that suits us better than slaughter."

"We will break them like they have never before been broken. But it serves us well to have servants," Morbin said, nodding at the crew of serving rabbits. "It's a family tradition," he said, looking at Gern, who cackled appreciatively.

"We are your allies, Lord Morbin," Flox said, bowing low, "now and always. We follow you to victory."

A cough sounded behind Sween. She panicked. *No, Melody.*

"You have something to say, slave?" Gern asked, peering past Sween to the young rabbit behind.

Melody coughed again.

"I can't hear you. Slave?" Gern repeated.

"Don't," Sween risked a whisper.

But Melody threw down her tray and rushed at Morbin, shattering glass as she cried out in defiance, "The Green Ember rises! The seed of the new world smolders—" She was just getting going when Morbin sprang, drawing his black sickle as he came. Sween shrank, closing her eyes.

An awful scream. A silence far worse.

Sween was frozen in place, horrified. She opened her eyes. All the rabbit slaves were still. Gritch ran in, bowing apologetically to Morbin, who had resumed his throne. He fell awkwardly to his knees beneath the grey rabbit. "My lord, please forgive me. I warned them."

A quick, powerful strike met the old rabbit's jaw, and he spun back. Sween remained frozen while Gritch stumbled to his feet and hobbled out of the room.

"Forgive me, Lord Morbin," the grey rabbit said, bowing low. He stood and resumed his casual confidence. "About the agreement. You were saying?"

"All is now ready," Morbin said. "The scheme is settled. It will stop this pathetic roiling. So long as my old rival is wounded again, even in his grave. But the price, Ambassador, is not open for negotiation. Do make that very clear."

"I will reiterate your terms," the grey rabbit said.

"Do," Morbin said, glancing to where Melody's body lay still. "I will hear no more of a Mended Wood or of Jupiter's heir."

Sween's heart sank. She filed out of the room along with the other slaves, head down and heart broken.

Through tears, she tried to remember the song. But in her troubled trembling, she had lost the words. She could not even recall the tune.

Chapter Thirty-Five

GREEN AND GOLD

Picket woke with a start. Shaking loose of his blanket, he rolled away from the still-burning fire and got to his feet. It was dark, and he had slept very little.

The wind was steady and cold, with occasional gusts. Picket liked that. He felt fresher than he had the day before. When he thought of what happened, a darkness brewed inside him. He forced his heart to build a dam against the flood of guilt and woe that threatened to overwhelm him. He must, as Uncle Wilfred said, carry his wounds—his own secret wounds—into the battle.

He rose to scan the camp. The mountains began to glow faintly with the approach of dawn. The captains were going from tent to tent, campfire to campfire, rousing the rabbits and forming them into companies. He saw Heyward at a near fire, bending over his stack of rods, threading them through a sturdy cloth. Picket was glad to see him in the catapult crews, where his gifts were so useful.

Captain Helmer limped up nearby, nodded solemnly to Picket, then pointed to the forest. Picket nodded, rubbed at his eyes, and set to work packing his few belongings. A young rabbit from the baggage unit came, took Picket's blankets, and helped him strap on his breastplate. Once there had been a clear double-diamond emblem on the simple armor, but it was faded now. As he settled it into place, he thought of Bleston, camped on the ridges above them, the Whitson Stone around his neck. He had pledged to give the ancient heirloom, this symbol and seal of royal authority, to Smalls. But would he give it now to Emma? Picket knew she ought to own it, along with the Green Ember. The two gems belonged together. Emma was the chosen heir and the rightful ruler.

When the youngster was done and had moved on to help others, Picket drew his sword. It had been a gift from the prince, from Smalls. It was an irreplaceable treasure to Picket, almost too valuable to use. But it was designed for battle, forged with sturdy steel. It was longer than his last sword and heavier, though with his growing strength, it no longer felt unwieldy. It felt like a deadly extension of his body.

He held the weapon out, laying the blade gently into his left hand as he held the hilt in his right. He gazed at the emblem on the pommel. It was a rabbit, sword in hand, with wings extended behind him. Picket had flown at Jupiter's Crossing, not far from where he now stood. He had launched from the back of an attacking bird, flipped in the air and kicked another, before descending like lightning on Redeye Garlackson. Afterward, in gratitude for that act of heroic courage, the prince had honored him with this sword. Picket had hoped to use it to help Smalls to the throne.

Had hoped.

They discussed the sword the last time they spoke. Smalls had shown him how the circular emblem popped out when you turned it a certain way, revealing a small secret compartment. And just before the prince left on his ill-fated journey to Kingston, he had given Picket something to keep there. Now Picket turned and popped the circular seal off, revealing the hidden compartment beneath. As the sun appeared on the horizon, bathing the valley in gold, Picket saw the emerald gem gleaming in the breaking dawn.

"If the worst should happen, Picket," the prince had said, "give this, with all my love, to my sister. Tell Emma that I believe in her, that I'm sorry I won't be there to see her crowned. Tell her, from me, that I'm sorry. Say whatever you think best when the time comes, Picket. And Heather," he had paused, looking away as his voice dropped to a whisper, "please take good care of Heather. I always hoped for—well, I always wished good things for Heather. I must leave now. But I entrust this relic of my family to you, my brother."

Picket closed the seal, concealing the hidden gem, and sheathed his sword. He looked to the rising dawn, breathed deeply, then set his jaw. His face was serious and settled, a furious storm curtained off by calm. For now. But the curtain would come down this day. He would be an arrow aimed at the heart of Morbin's forces.

He turned toward the forest just as Jo and Cole came striding in beside him. The three of them went silently, sunlight playing over their faces, until they moved into the forest with hundreds of others.

"We go," Picket said as they set off beneath the canopy of trees, "back to Jupiter's Crossing."

Chapter Thirty-Six

A LIVING QUEEN

Heather came slowly awake, lost in an eerie, frightening dream. In the dream she had been a little child again, playing among the trees of Nick Hollow. At first it had been pleasant, but the dream turned dark when she lost something she couldn't name, something she had been charged to keep safe.

The dream continued with her running through East Wood. In the dream, the wood was a forbidden, frightening collection of decaying trees. The trees grabbed at her, cackling in the growing darkness as burning limbs fell all around her. She looked up as a fiery brand fell, hurled by a sneering black bird with a golden crown and a long black sickle in his grip. "Bear the flame!" he screeched.

She fell, crashing through the surface of the ground and landing in a dank underground hollow thick with fog. Large eggs covered the ground all around her, and a slick whispering voice sounded in her ears. "They will awaken," it said.

She struggled to stand but couldn't move. She wanted to cry out, but her voice would make no sound. Then she saw him. Smalls lay motionless beside her. The dream ended as her necklace caught fire and a scaly hand found her in the fog.

She had always had dreams, including bad ones, and they seemed to be getting worse. Back home, when she had a bad dream, she would crawl into bed beside her mother. And Mother would sing. No better tonic existed, and Heather's heart would swell with every sweet, soft note in the night. She would feel safe again, safe and hopeful and glad.

But Mother was gone. She might never hear her mother's voice again.

Heather shook her head, willing the memory of the dream away, then sat up. Feeling for her necklace, she found that the torch charm was cool. She blinked and gazed at the painting on the wall at the end of her bed. It was a lovely glen in the Great Wood, in the time before the fall of King Jupiter Goodson. This was, she believed, her family's lost home, a home where she knew she belonged, though she had never seen it. At least if she *had* seen this place, it had been when she was a baby, and she had no memory of it. Still, her heart ached for it.

She sighed. The Mended Wood seemed so far away. Today would tip the balance in one direction or another. After today, the Mended Wood would either become a legend for a lost cause, a sad song for a few faithful exiles and slaves, or grow ever closer to reality.

Heather had a part to play. The ragged edges of the awful dream faded away, and she sprang out of bed. She was grateful that she had been quartered in her and Picket's old familiar room in the stone corridors of Cloud Mountain. She got dressed, eager to do her part for Emma's cause, for the warriors in the field, and for the community she loved.

In honor of Smalls.

For the Mended Wood.

She hurried down the corridor and up the stairs, through King's Garden and Hallway Round.

Entering the great hall, she found Emma working on her tonic and instructing the hospital volunteers in how to help evaluate and dose the wounded. Doctor Zeiger stood nearby, huddled with the surgeons and barbers, their grisly tools at the ready as the old doctor talked them through what to expect. Not far off, Eefaw Potter was spinning his wheel, forging every kind of clay vessel the medical staff needed to prepare for the battle. Smiling wide, he waved at her, unwittingly slinging mud on a passing nurse, then quickly reached again for the wet clay that had begun to fly free of his wheel. Heather smiled and waved back.

She worried that she had slept longer than she meant to, but when Emma saw her, she called out, "Doctor Longtreader is here. Come up here, Heather. Don't worry; we've only just started. Doctor Longtreader knows this tonic as well as I do, so she will be in charge here while I help Doctor Zeiger with the surgery. Any questions?"

"What do we do if we run out?" a young rabbit asked. Heather recognized her as Gloria Folds, the young apprentice of Garden Mistress Halmond.

"We do the best we can, Gloria," Heather said. "We'll dose on the conservative side to begin with and, together with the more experienced doctors, evaluate patients who need more urgent care. The barbers will sew up wounds, and the surgeons will treat the worst cases. You all will be a tremendous help to us, but don't take on more than you need to. Just do your part, and it will help. Doctor Emma and the others will show us the way."

Emma smiled weakly, but with affection, at Heather, then turned back to the volunteers. "Now, if all has gone as planned, our soldiers will be in great peril very soon. We have all, I hope, gotten some rest. We will need all our strength. It may be a while before we can rest again. So I'm ordering you all to take half an hour. Go. Find a peaceful spot. Talk with your friends or family. If you need solitude, find a place to be alone. Meditate, clear your head, speak to a votary or a wise friend. Be back here in half an hour, ready to work."

The team broke up slowly, heading off to find a moment of peace before the battle.

Heather wrapped Emma in a tender embrace. They said nothing for a few moments. Then Emma pulled back. "Can we walk together, Heather?" she asked. "One last time?"

"One last time?" Heather asked. "My dear Emma, we may yet win this."

Emma nodded, her eyes cast down. "I suppose we have to believe that."

"Picket's out there," Heather said. "I have to believe it."

"Yes, dear old Shuffler," she said, and they laughed at the memory of Emma's teasing name for Picket. "I pray he comes through this awful day. I'm worried for him, but now I must think of all of them. I must love them all in a way I didn't, couldn't have, yesterday."

"It's a terrible burden to have thrust on you so suddenly," Heather said. "Emma, you won't believe how I longed to tell you. I was in pieces worrying about keeping it from you."

"I spoke with my father—I mean with Lord Rake—for a time last night. I understand why you had to do it. It was wise. And I am, I believe, strong enough to know who I am. It has relieved a long-simmering sorrow."

"You are very brave."

"I am brave, yes. But I'm also afraid."

"Are you afraid of what happens if we lose?"

"Yes, but perhaps more afraid of what happens if we win."

"You will be our queen," Heather said, fighting back tears, "the one in whom we hope."

"I think," Emma said, "that you were better prepared for that life than I will ever be."

They walked on, saying little as they crossed out of the hall, till Heather realized they were headed for the mossy porch. A blast of cool wind met them as they opened the door. Heather flinched. She followed Emma down the stairs, along the porch, and up to where an old rabbit sat mending clothes. She kept at her work, sewing with remarkable speed. Beside her lay heaps of baskets, a long spyglass, and an extinguished candle.

"Mrs. Weaver?" Emma asked. "May we speak to you for a moment?"

"Of course, my dears," she said, finishing up a torn shirt. She looked up, then rose and hugged each of them in turn. She stayed on her feet, stretching. "It's been a while, girls, and you've been through quite a lot."

"We have," Heather said, nodding as they sat. "Especially Emma."

"You mean Her Royal Highness," Mrs. Weaver said, easing down onto her knees.

"Mrs. Weaver, please," Emma said, moving to help the old rabbit up.

"Ah, ah, young lady," Mrs. Weaver said, shooing her away with insistent gestures. "You must be who you are, Princess, for no one else can be. And further, you must let me be who I am."

"Yes, ma'am," Emma said.

"So, you know?" Heather asked, as she helped Mrs. Weaver slowly to her feet.

"Know what?" the wise old rabbit asked as she settled back into her chair. "That the king and queen had a secret youngest daughter hidden away on Cloud Mountain? You could say that." She raised her eyebrows and smiled.

"You knew before yesterday," Heather said.

"I did, child. It was my idea."

"Your idea?" Emma said. "Who decided this? Was it just you and the lords?"

"There were only a few of us in council—how I got there is an odd story, but for another time—and I made the suggestion. Your mother, though it pained her, agreed with my counsel, and that's when Lord Rake took you as his own. In fact, that's when this horrid business of me being called 'Maggie O'Sage' started. That was the queen's fault."

"You knew my mother?" Emma asked, scooting to the edge of her seat. "What was she like?"

"Knew her?" Mrs. Weaver said. "I know her. And besides her annoying habit of giving rabbits grand titles that they hate and can't ever seem to shake off, the queen is a good lady."

"She *is*?" Emma began.

"Dear Princess Emma," Mrs. Weaver said, "your mother is still alive."

Chapter Thirty-Seven

RETREAT AT JUPITER'S CROSSING

Picket huddled with his fellow soldiers on the edge of the clearing known as Jupiter's Crossing. The battle would begin on this hallowed ground. He glanced along the lines and saw several small teams huddled as they were. Other officers, though none as young as Picket, were leading their own small bands.

Picket bent to whisper. "Remember the plan, bucks. Surge out and sail into them, but listen for the order. Listen hard. And only pass on what you hear from an officer. Be sharp, and do what damage you can. Stay tight and follow orders."

The huddled bucks, including Jo and Cole, nodded solemnly. Picket saw the eagerness in their eyes, the fear and focus. He extended a fist into the midst of the circle of rabbits. "For Jupiter's heir and Jupiter's blood," he said.

They put their fists into the center of the circle. When they withdrew them, they placed them over their hearts.

"My place beside you, my blood for yours. Till the Green Ember rises, or the end of the world!"

They turned and crept to the forest edge. An army of well-provisioned wolves stood on the opposite side of the crossing, their camp extending to the center of the field.

"Just where they're supposed to be," Cole whispered. Picket nodded, remembering many months before when he had saved Smalls very near here. How he wished Smalls were with them now.

Jo was securing his weapons. His tightly belted quiver was teeming with arrows. He had a catch he could loose to free the arrows for easy drawing, but for now it was locked down to free his movements. Each arrow was precious. He didn't want to lose a single one in the wild close combat to come.

Peering down the line of trees beside him, Picket spotted Helmer. The old captain glanced both ways, then nodded.

Picket inhaled, squaring his shoulders to the clearing. He drew his sword and absently fingered the circular seal with its flying rabbit emblem. *For you, Smalls. For you I'll fly into battle today. With this gift, I'll do my best to secure a future for your sister and for all her subjects.*

Helmer shouted, "For the Mended Wood!" and ran into the clearing. Half a step behind, hundreds of rabbits broke from the tree line and sprinted out beside him. Picket was one of the first. Cole bared his own blade in stride and let out a fierce war cry, while Jo surged forward, nocking a free arrow as he came.

The wolves were surprised but quickly formed a battle line. They were eager when the clash came. Picket reached the foremost wolves and drove in with ferocious zeal. His towering sword met a raised spear shaft, and his blade cleaved it in two.

Picket launched onto his opponent, picked out of the scores before him, and fought like he had never fought before. His blood was up, his mind alert, and his limbs felt charged. Blocking one spear thrust, he hopped forward to evade another. He landed on the shaft, and it shattered as he came surging on, battling the wolf warrior till he was defeated.

Picket turned in time to see a sword swing for his middle. He reacted with poise, bringing his own sword around to deflect the enemy's blade. With quick motions, he warded off three more stabs. Then he attacked, ending another enemy.

Now three grisly wolves struck at Picket at once. He gritted his teeth and sliced out, catching one and sending him sprawling. But the others were on him. One leapt, knocking into him and sending him rolling back to collide with a large cart's wheel. A bloody gash appeared along his cheek. As Picket tried to regain his footing, the wolf pounced. No time. He arced toward Picket with a bloodthirsty gaze. Picket tried to bring his blade around, but too slowly. It was too late.

The wolf flew at him, all teeth and fury.

Just as the wolf's breath was on his neck, he careened sideways, intercepted by desperate crashing kicks from Cole and Jo. Picket leapt up, swinging his sword to defend his friends as they recovered their feet. Jo checked his quiver. Still tight and not an arrow missing. Cole recovered, ripping his sword free and repeating his bellowing cry as the black buck waded into the battle beside his friends.

Jo leapt backward, flipping in an arc to land on the cart, drawing an arrow as he landed. From atop his perch on the wagon, he shot the wolf nearest Picket. The arrow sent him stumbling back to crumple and stir no more. Unhooking the catch on his quiver, Jo sent a series of deadly darts into the ravenous band of wolves.

The battle-wild wolves were enraged. They came for Jo with a slavering fury. Picket and Cole took up the defense of the cart, rallying more rabbits to preserve this advantage.

They battled on, Jo raining arrows, until the wolf commanders sent in arrows of their own. After a wild minute, they surrendered the cart and, under Picket's command, re-formed a little ways off. They battled on, forming a wall of blades that chewed into the enemy. But they were no longer surging ahead. They were losing too many rabbits.

Picket stood as tall as he could, ears attentive. A spear point broke the line and cut a deep gash in his arm. Gritting his teeth against the pain, he fought on. His sword found another wolf attacker as a shout rang through the ranks.

It was Helmer. He was crying out, and the other officers and soldiers were passing on the call.

"Retreat!"

Picket turned toward his company. "Retreat!" he shouted, turning his tail to the wolves and sprinting into the forest.

They fled, surrendering the sacred soil of Jupiter's Crossing amid the jeering, jubilant shouts of the wolf army.

Chapter Thirty-Eight

TRAPS

My mother is alive?" Emma asked.

"Yes," Mrs. Weaver said, smiling. "She's been alive her whole life. She has lived for many years near Kingston, in a hidden glen."

"The Lady of the Glen?" Heather asked, her eyes widening. "I met her! She came to my home, in Nick Hollow."

Emma was flustered, searching for words. "Then why," she began, "what is the...?"

Heather asked what Emma could not. "Then why isn't she queen? She's called the queen, right? Why isn't she ruling? I mean, I would dearly love to hear that my own mother was still alive and hear her voice again, but why isn't Lady Glen ruling?"

"It's a good question but answered simply enough," Mrs. Weaver said. "She can't be the monarch. She has no royal blood, is not a descendant of King Whitson. She's really a royal consort, but she's called queen by courtesy and custom. When you are crowned, Princess Emma, she will be the Queen Mother."

"But why," Emma began, tears in her eyes, "has she never come to me? Why has she been a stranger to me my whole life?"

"I'm sorry, dear," Mrs. Weaver answered. "It's because of my scheme, my idea to keep you secret. She did, when you were much smaller, come and hold you in the night. She loves you very much, child. And perhaps your reunion is near."

Emma's brows knit. "I have some vague memories of a grey lady holding me."

Mrs. Weaver nodded, her eyes sad.

The far door burst open, and Lord Rake strode onto the porch, followed by Pacer. "Your Highness," he said, bowing to Emma. "Doctor Longtreader."

"Lord Rake," Emma said, nodding respectfully.

"Your Highness, the battle is joined."

"Then we all have work to do," she said.

"Maggie," Lord Rake said, "are you prepared?"

The wise rabbit nodded, reaching back to remove stacks of clothing from a large barrel. A cloth was stuffed into a hole near the top, and Mrs. Weaver lifted a flint-and-steel from a hidden pocket. "I'm ready."

"What's this?" Emma asked.

Mrs. Weaver stood while Lord Rake and Pacer moved the rocking chair and the rug beneath it. A trapdoor was revealed.

"I'm more than just a mad old rabbit sewing on a porch and staring longingly into the fog," she said. Heather offered

Mrs. Weaver her hand for balance. "I'm also the guardian of one of the few secret passages into Cloud Mountain."

"And before we'll let the enemy in this door…" Lord Rake said, nodding to the barrel.

"Kaboom," Mrs. Weaver said, a mischievous smile spreading over her face. "There are many mysterious passages in this place. For this one, I am the guardian. Would you like to know of some others?"

* * *

Picket raced through the trees, turning at intervals to track the wolf pursuit. Some rabbits were being overtaken, but most were far enough ahead to bring off their harried escape. Cutting through the familiar forest, the bands of rabbits came together to form one fast fleeing army. Helmer and Picket fell into a sprinting stride together; the older rabbit hobbled slightly but did not slow the retreat.

A soldier nearby cried in panic, "They'll catch us!"

"Press on, Mitchell," Helmer shouted. "Keep your eyes ahead, bucks!"

The rabbits reached the forest edge and poured into the clearing where they'd camped the night before. This was Rockback Valley, a long, narrow field blocked at the rear by the sheer base of Cloud Mountain. There were several easy paths up the mountain, but this wasn't one of them. Here the mountainside was high and rocky, a difficult ascent, even for small groups of rabbits. For an army, it was impossible.

The rabbit camp was settled in this way, blocked behind by the towering mountain and flanked beside by the forest, which now teemed with attacking wolves. Before the camp lay the long, narrow valley that led to the small plain where Morbin's forces massed.

The fleeing rabbits had run into a trap.

Chapter Thirty-Nine

THE BATTLE OF ROCKBACK VALLEY BEGINS

Picket and Helmer led their battle-tested force into the camp, moving behind the lines of fresh rabbits, now formed in rigid ranks. They passed line after line of ready soldiers armed with bows, arrows, and swords. The waiting troops nodded with respect to the returning bands.

Re-forming in the back of the rested troops, the gasping rabbits caught their breath, and some received treatment from medics. Picket's band settled in near the catapults and blastpowder barrels that lay along the rock wall. Rockback Valley's namesake cliff was a menacing feature. There was no going any farther back.

The cold wind felt good on Picket's face as he cleaned his blade and accepted a swallow of water from the young buck who'd taken his baggage earlier. Picket thanked him, then noticed blue-robed Heyward, doing his part to crank down the arm of the nearest catapult. The massive arm lowered slowly with a persistent click and a rattle. He could see the wood straining under the pressure as a blastpowder keg was placed in the sling.

A field medic came to stitch the gash on Picket's arm, another to wipe the wound on his face. Helmer had crossed to confer with the catapult captain. Nodding to the captain, the old black rabbit held up his hand and scanned the tree line.

"Hold!" he commanded, his teeth set in a snarl.

There was no enemy in sight, but sounds of scuffling and snarling issued from the cover of the trees. The wolves seemed to be gathering into attack formations. Picket gritted his teeth while the medic began to stitch his wound. He watched as the other two catapults were prepped and loaded with blastpowder barrels, each with a cloth stuffed in a hole at the top. Rabbits with torches stood by, nervously eying Captain Helmer and the dark edge of the forest. Picket focused on the forest.

Waiting. Watching.

The wolves came in packs, howling and barking. They broke through the trees and charged the poised rabbits.

Helmer cried out, "Fire away!" and dropped his hand.

The barrel cloths were lit and the catapult slings tripped. Each of the great arms leapt forward, slamming into their corrals as their cargo flew far and high toward the enemy. The wolves looked up in time to see three barrels sailing toward them. One exploded in the air, sending a shattering echo through the valley. The flame from its blast caught the other two barrels just as they struck the enemy line. They shattered in a death-dealing spray of fire and shrapnel.

The rabbit lines sent up a shout, their fists in the air. But the steady archers in front made careful aim. At Captain Frye's rasped command, they loosed a volley of arrows on the advancing wolves.

Now a new kind of howling sounded from the wolf ranks. The attack slowed as the wolves looked back to see the damage done. They skidded to a halt, torn between their ravenous hunger for battle and the reality that they were, for the moment, cut off from support. Some came ahead, meeting eager opponents who dispatched them efficiently. Many turned back.

The rabbits shouted again as the bulk of the wolf force tried to re-form behind the tree line. Picket knew there were great numbers of wolves coming from that side. Still more would come, far more than they could handle. He looked ahead, to the open valley, peering into the distance with keen eyes.

"They'll come," Cole said. "We'll be overmatched ten to one and backed against the cliff."

"Have some faith," Picket said, glancing at the medic who was still trying to close his long gash.

He looked at Heyward and saw the catapult teams repositioning two of the machines. The turning went slowly, so Picket called for help and, ignoring the protests of the medic, fell in beside Heyward, straining under the effort of moving the great machine. After more help arrived, Heyward stepped back, eyeballing the orientation of the catapult in relation to its intended target.

"Hold!" Heyward cried, and the rabbits stopped.

"Brother Heyward," Picket said, clasping hands with his old friend and nodding to the flaming wreck in the forest to their right. "I think you've found your calling."

"I can help with this, to be sure. But I've worked on other things," he said. "I wish we had more time. I've made something I'd love for you—"

He was cut off by a growing murmur in the ranks. Picket pointed ahead. The forward force of Morbin's army appeared over the near hill. The army was huge, its ranks swollen with marching wolves. Over it, the sky was dark.

The Lords of Prey had come.

Picket couldn't say if Morbin was in their number. He hoped he was.

"Okay," Helmer said. "We've done our part. Now if Bleston will do his, we may have a chance."

Chapter Forty

THE TENTH WINDOW

Heather and Emma followed Lord Rake and his attendants as they quit the foggy porch, leaving Mrs. Weaver at her vigil over the secret door. Lord Rake gave orders to Pacer, who nodded and ran into the great hall. He turned to Emma.

"The battle is on, Your Highness," he said, "but you still have some time to do what you will before the first wounded arrive. Everything will change after today." He looked into her eyes, and his voice quavered. "I have tried, my dear, to do the best I could for you. I never wanted you to find out this way. I wanted it to be happy news after the war was won, with your brother on the throne and you a princess in the Mended Wood. I'm sorry it could not be so. But know this," he said, "I shall always love you like my own. Today I fight for the Mended Wood, and for the community I cherish. But no cause is greater than my love for you. I fight because you are in my heart."

"My father," she said, rushing into his arms.

Nothing more was said. After a long moment, Lord Rake turned and, wiping his eyes, hurried through the door.

Emma and Heather were left in Hallway Round, alone but for the guards at the blastpowder barrels. Then doors opened and groups of busy rabbits hurried through. Urgent noises filled the hallway.

Heather turned to Emma. "What can I do for you?" she asked. "What do you need?"

"Perhaps a private place," Emma answered, sniffing, "a quiet place for just a moment's peace."

"Follow me," Heather said, taking Emma's hand.

In a moment they were entering Lighthall. Heather checked to see if anyone was inside. When she saw no one, she hugged Emma and headed for the door. "I'll be out here, whenever you're ready."

"Stay. Please," Emma said, and Heather nodded, following her inside.

Lighthall was a lovely rounded room, wood-walled with colored light shining through ten enormous windows. The light spread over the polished wood floors, and bright beams appeared in columns from overhead ports. The windows that surrounded the wondrous room told tales of King Jupiter's storied reign. Heather had first thought of this place as the Room of Ten Tales, and in fact each window had several scenes, one large and central, with others surrounding it. Here were murals marking the golden age of rabbitkind, the zenith of the culture begun by Flint and Fay in the Blue Moss Hills, carried on through the centuries on Golden

Coast, and then finally here in Natalia. King Jupiter's coronation and early battles were depicted beautifully, and all was glory until the ninth window revealed a horrific scene. The fall of King Jupiter. The afterterrors. Emma walked past it.

Heather looked up at the images and, seeing Morbin Blackhawk perched triumphantly over the slain body of King Jupiter, she was seized by indignation. She stared, thinking of all the faithful who had fallen since that awful day at Jupiter's Crossing.

She didn't want to look at the tenth window, but she did. Emma was already kneeling beneath the breathtaking scene. It showed Smalls, as he would have been, crowned and glorious, reigning over the Mended Wood. It was a vision of hope, expertly crafted, imagining the glories of a new world. Hot tears came. Heather fell to her knees beside Emma.

Neither said anything for several minutes. Heather thought of all that was lost in a world without Smalls. Her own sorrows, great as they were, must be dim in comparison with Emma's. She draped an arm around her friend and felt the sobs beginning to shake the princess. Heather clasped her tighter, reaching to hold Emma as she wept.

"I will come through this," Emma said. "But I had to walk into it and feel the weight of it all."

"Of course, Emma," she said. "I can't imagine what you're going through."

"You can imagine it, Heather. That's why I'm so grateful to have you by my side."

"I will never abandon you. Commoner or queen, I am your friend. For life, or death, I'll be faithful."

"Thank you, Heather. I know you had hoped for more, that my brother meant so much to you. You knew him far better than I."

"We had been through a lot together, and I had hoped there were more adventures ahead. He was a great rabbit," Heather said, staring up at his heroic image.

There was a scuffling commotion behind them—hurried footsteps, the twang of a bowstring. An arrow sped overhead, shattering the glass of the tenth window. Heather screamed. Emma jumped back as the idyllic scene fell in a crystal cascade. Heather leapt to cover Emma, to protect her from the falling glass.

Wide-eyed and terrified, she spun to see who had done this.

On the other side of Lighthall, Bleston lowered his bow.

Chapter Forty-One

Stepping Forward

Picket watched them spill over the ridge, and his breath caught in his chest.

Morbin's army was enormous.

They marched in time, sharp and imposing. Picket knew that wolves naturally lacked discipline, that their bloodlust often overcame their self-control and ability to follow orders in a strategic battle plan. This was a vulnerability wise rabbit commanders would use against them. But under Morbin's banner, marching in concert beneath a sky of hawks, eagles, and more, these wolves moved in tight, restrained units. As they marched closer, he could see the bloodlust in their faces. They were the same wild and vicious enemies, only harnessed to attack with military precision.

The untested troops in the front of the rabbit army seemed to wither at the sight. But Picket funneled his dread into grim determination, then a furious resolve. The exasperated medic ran up to him and set to work on his wounded arm again.

"We'll be slaughtered!" a soldier said. "There are too many," another added. A grumbling spread through the ranks. These soldiers were brave, but not stupid, and the menacing force massed against them made for an impossible contest. They knew it. The feeling was spreading. "We can't win!"

Picket frowned. Shaking free of the medic, he marched forward. His face was set, his eyes hard, and all his movements sure. Step by step, he passed the whispering, fearful, murmuring ranks. Many rabbits recognized him and whispered. "Picket Longtreader, the hero of Jupiter's Crossing. The youngest lieutenant in the army, and Prince Smalls' particular friend." Scores of clean-clothed soldiers watched as this dirty, sweat-drenched rabbit, blood trickling down his cheek and soaking the fur of his arm, walked purposefully to the head of the army as Morbin's forces came on.

Cole and Jo fell in behind him, bearing their own wounds, and other soldiers from the early fight followed. As they pushed ahead, the complaints died down. Picket reached the front of the army and kept going, moving well ahead of the front line.

His fellows fell in behind him, bloody marks of their earlier battle plain. The medic had followed Picket and now came for him, trying to finish the job stitching his arm. Picket turned once, and his withering glare sent the medic hurrying back to his place. Picket turned to face the enemy.

His face was set like steel, his body composed in a clear, rock-hard resolve.

Now the rabbit ranks fell silent. The silence stretched over seconds. Then an old sergeant on what had been the front line, a grey campaigner of many wars, began to laugh. "All right," he said, smiling. "All right, bucks!" And he walked forward. Soon his fellows were joining him, and the lines of troops, embarrassed by their distance from Picket's ragged band, rushed to form up just behind them. Row on row, the rabbits advanced. A different sort of murmur swelled, and soon the call of "All right, bucks!" was bouncing around the army.

Picket never said a word, only drew his sword and pointed it at the oncoming army.

The wolves in the fore stopped, eyes flitting from their commanders to the rabbit host. Trapped rabbits. Vulnerable rabbits. Easy pickings. Some of the wolves made to advance, but a harsh bark from their commander held them in place.

Overhead, the Lords of Prey circled. The sky teemed with winged warriors, their breasts armored, their feet gripping cruel blades. These raptors were ready for battle. Picket regarded them. They were close enough now that he could make out their faces and hear their brash calls.

The wolf commander looked up at a circling eagle. He was white-furred and muscular, clad in black with a black shield. The shield was old-fashioned, possibly an heirloom. It was wooden, painted in black and bearing the sign of a bright red fang jutting from a deformed diamond. It was a mockery of the rabbits' cherished Whitson Stone. The eagle above was brown, with a splash of white showing around the edges of his black helm. In his feet he bore weapons—a sharp short sword and a spiked mallet.

"At Lord Gern's command!" the white wolf shouted. His eager soldiers, tongues lolling, shivered with anticipation.

Picket nodded. *Gern, Morbin's chief lieutenant. The architect of the afterterrors that ruined the Great Wood.* He eyed the bird with careful attention, marking all he could in the few moments he had. Then Picket looked back at Captain Frye, a question in his young eyes. The old soldier nodded, an understanding clear between them. Picket looked up at Gern, then over at the wolf commander. The white wolf raised his shield, awaiting the signal.

Picket didn't wait.

He broke into a sprint, surprising even Cole and Jo, who followed quickly with their bloody band of brave rabbits. The first ranks of the army followed fast, crying out as they came.

The rabbits, trapped in an impossible position, outnumbered and without a chance, were charging the wolf and raptor army with defiant shouts.

Picket watched as Gern banked suddenly and let loose a piercing call, then swooped to the back as the wolf commander cried out, "Attack!"

But they were *being* attacked. Picket's band clashed with the edges of the wolf army as the birds of prey descended.

"Away!" came another cry, then an explosion overhead. Two more explosions. The blastpowder barrels had blown

in the air, shielding the rabbits from the swooping raptors. These fell back, while wolves and rabbits clashed below the smoke and fire.

Picket ran straight for the wolf commander. In the white wolf's face he saw disbelief, then alarm, then an eager anger. His soldiers had moved ahead of him, but he drew up his spear and howled.

Picket charged the front lines at top speed, and, spying the white wolf behind a packed band of warriors, he leapt.

Chapter Forty-Two

THE EMPTY RIDGE

Picket's leap took the wolves by surprise, but they rallied, aiming their spears at the foolhardy soaring rabbit. Then Cole was there with an eager band, and they cut down the first wolves in a furious assault. Arcing over the front line, Picket bore down on the white wolf, who swiveled his spear toward Picket as he descended. But a speeding arrow found the spearhead and knocked it aside. Picket crashed onto the stunned wolf's shield, breaking it in two with a shattering kick.

Jo reloaded his bow and fired again.

Picket blocked a return thrust from the white wolf, then fell on him with a fury. They went to the ground in a swirling dust storm, but only one rose to his feet again.

Seeing their commander slain, the wolves went mad with rage.

Picket swiveled, finding new foes and more work for his deadly weapon. Cole was struck from behind and crashed hard to the ground. Picket leapt in front of his friend, but the frenzied wolf knocked him on his back.

"Lieutenant!" came the shout, as Lallo and three of his fellow soldiers sailed into the wolf. They beat him back as more rabbits poured in from behind. Finding his feet, Picket took a moment to survey the scene. The brave surge from the foremost rabbits had disrupted the wolf attack, but more wolves flooded in from the woods. The small band that met them, commanded by Captain Frye, could not last long. The main line was turning, and Morbin's army had every advantage. The sky was clearing of smoke. Raptors descended on the rabbits behind the lines, and, hard as the rabbits fought, they had no defense.

Picket looked to the ridges above and, seeing nothing, his heart sank.

Where is Bleston?

The catapults, under Helmer's command, were their only hope against the deadly birds of prey.

"Jo!" Picket shouted as the soldier sent arrow after arrow into the wolf army. "To Helmer!" he called. Cole joined them, and the three hurried toward the catapults.

The wolves that had broken this far behind their lines were fighting alone. Together, Picket, Jo, and Cole made a difficult band for any single wolf to defeat. But it wasn't long before Picket heard the swishing of wings above him, and turning, he saw a hawk closing in.

The small band of rabbits dropped to their backs on the ground, their blades jutting up like deadly nettles. Jo sent his arrows flying, but the hawk dodged and dipped as he descended. He hovered above them, beating his wings and slashing with a long sword. Picket barely dodged the cleaving swipe. He rolled over as the blade cut a long furrow in the dirt. Picket gasped, gazing up at the hawk with wide eyes.

He was out of ideas.

The hawk cackled, brought his blade around, and beat his wings. He was ready to strike. But he was struck by a speeding barrel. *The catapults!* The bird spun, then spiraled down to crash into a pair of advancing wolves. The barrel dropped and landed, lit but unexploded, right where Picket, Cole, and Jo lay sprawling. The fire was inching closer to the keg.

Terrified, the three rabbits scrambled to their feet and fled. The keg exploded behind them. There was a flash of light—a bright blazing orange rimmed in gold. The concussive wave hit Picket, sending him crashing down to fall in a heap, his fur singed and head aching.

Shaking his head, he rose slowly to his feet. At first, he could hear nothing. His head pounded and his ears rang.

Shaking off the pain and confusion, he ran for the catapults. But Cole, looking singed and battered himself, grabbed his arm and led him back. Picket had been running the wrong way.

As the ringing in his ears subsided and the sounds of battle slowly returned, Picket realized he was wounded, bleeding in several places. But his mind had cleared by the time they reached Helmer. Along with Heyward and a band of soldiers, Helmer was working furiously to reload the third catapult. Archers stood nearby, firing in disciplined squads, holding off the circling raptors.

"Thanks for that!" Picket shouted at Helmer.

"That was Heyward!" Helmer shouted back. Heyward saluted, then resumed his work cranking down the catapult arm. When it was ready and had been carefully aimed by Heyward, Helmer shouted, "Fire!" The barrel was lit and sent aloft as the arm came forward in a shattering crack. The giant wooden arm sent its cargo into the sky to burst in a terrific blaze. But the arm came apart in a rending split that sheared it in half.

"It's useless, sir!" Heyward cried, quickly examining the broken arm. "No possibility of fixing it here."

"That leaves us with two," Helmer said, shaking his head.

"Where's Bleston?" Picket shouted, glancing to the ridge above. "He's supposed to be here by now! What's happened to the plan?"

Helmer turned to Picket. "Can't you see? Bleston's not coming."

Picket turned toward the empty ridge. Bleston was supposed to bring his force in on the flank, slamming into the unsuspecting enemy army. His large force would have given the rabbits at least some chance. And they had hoped for reinforcements from Cloud Mountain and more catapult support from above.

But no one was going to help them. They were trapped, alone, driven against the rocks.

"The outlet?" Heyward asked, frowning. There was a small escape point between the forest and the mountain, a last avenue of retreat in case the worst happened.

"We just got a runner back," Helmer said, shaking his head. "The pass is blocked by wolves. We're trapped. We wanted them to think we were, and, thanks to Bleston's treachery, we are."

"Betrayed," Picket said. "We are betrayed."

Chapter Forty-Three

BLOOD AND PEACE

Heather reeled. The tenth window lay scattered in shards at her feet. The beautiful vision of Smalls and the Mended Wood was shattered. She glowered at Bleston, who nocked another arrow and raised it.

Bleston smiled. Others came to stand beside him. Several of his Terralain guards were there, swords drawn, and last of all came Perkinson.

Perkinson? For a moment she was confused.

"Come with us, Emma," Bleston said.

"What is happening?" Heather asked.

Bleston said nothing, only motioned for Emma to come.

"You know who I am, and I stand in Kyle's way," Emma said. Heather wasn't sure how Emma felt, but her own heart was racing, and a hot anger grew within her.

"You liar!" Heather screamed, stepping in front of Emma. "You're a coward, Bleston Turncoat!"

She realized now that Bleston had never meant to swear fealty to Smalls, that everything he had done was a ruse to betray them. The weight of the betrayal came crashing down on her. Bleston was here, so he wasn't on the battlefield. That meant Picket and the army were stranded. Exposed. Hopeless. Bleston had planned their destruction. When they found Uncle Wilfred, Perkinson had learned about Smalls' death, and about Emma. And since he was clearly an agent for Bleston, he had reported to his master as soon as he could.

Emma was calculating as well. "All you have to do is get rid of me, and the throne is yours."

Bleston smiled. "Come with me, Emma."

"So the Silver Prince has stooped to this?" Heather spat.

"I will be remembered with honor," Bleston said, his face growing grave, "like all my honored ancestors."

"You are more dragon king than true heir to King Whitson. You will make yourself remembered, yes. They will call you the Sliver Prince."

"I'll take Emma either way," Bleston said, his eyes flashing. "But you have a choice to live or die."

"Perk," Heather said, "are you going to stand there while they kill her?"

"I'm not going to kill her," Bleston said.

"Of course, we can trust you," Heather said.

"I'm going to hand her over," he answered, "and Morbin will decide her fate."

Emma didn't move. Heather stood in front of her. "So you've done it again," Heather said. "You've spat on your father's grave and betrayed the true heir again."

"Come with us, Emma," Bleston said, his voice hardening,

"and we'll let Heather go. If you don't, she dies now."

"Never!" Heather spat. "Where she goes, I go."

"Heather, don't make this any harder," Perkinson said.

"You vile scum of rabbitkind," Heather said. "Your father would be ashamed of you. Perkin One-Eye was King Jupiter's best friend. Now his son has betrayed Jupiter's heir. How far back does your duplicity go?"

"He was Bleston's agent," Emma said, "must have been, even before he came to us at Halfwind."

"I have served King Bleston for many years," Perkinson said. "I'm not ashamed of my actions."

"And that's all we need to know about you," Heather said. "I should have known that Kyle could never change. I was a fool to trust any of you."

"Prince Kylen doesn't know about this. He's not even—" Perkinson began, but Bleston cut him off.

"That's enough, Perkinson. You've been faithful to me through hard days and you've done hard things, but leave this to me."

A horrible thought struck Heather. "Lord Ramnor!" she shouted, pointing to Perkinson. "You killed him. Before I got there, on the day of the attack. You killed him. He tried to tell me."

"I did what needed to be done," Perkinson said.

"Enough!" Bleston cried. "Now, Emma. Please come along," he said, pulling back his bowstring. "Or does Miss Longtreader have to die here, as her brother will die on the field?"

Emma stepped out from behind Heather. "I will go with you."

"No!" Heather cried.

"What choice do we have?" Emma answered.

"This," Heather said. After a deep breath, she sprinted to the eighth window and leapt into it. The glass shattered as she broke through.

Emma's eyes widened, but it took her only a fraction of a second to follow. An arrow whizzed past her as she dashed into the shattered space, leaping through on Heather's heels.

Heather landed, rolling on the ground before finding her feet. She was on a rocky path leading to the mouth of a cave. Emma landed behind her, and the two rabbits dashed ahead.

"This leads to the village green," Heather shouted, recalling Mrs. Weaver's revelation of several secret paths. "Just keep running!"

They ran down slick stone walkways until they emerged into the cave tunnel. Heather recognized it as the one leading to the staging platform. She knew that Emma's only chance for survival was on that plateau.

They reached the end of the passage and emerged, squinting, into daylight. Heather thought it odd that she couldn't hear anything. If the battle was on, where were the sounds of flying arrows and the noise of Lord Rake's catapults? At last her eyes adjusted to the light, and what she saw made her gasp. Lord Rake stood with his hands clasped behind his head, an angry scowl on his face. He was surrounded by archers in black with arrows carefully trained on him.

He saw Emma, and his eyes widened. "They said they had you, Emma, that if I lifted a finger to aid the battle, they would kill you. But now—"

"Now," said a rabbit in a grey hooded cloak, who stepped out from behind the archers. "Now, we do have her." He motioned for some of the archers to turn their arrows on Emma. "If you lift a finger to help her, or your battered comrades on the field below, we will kill her faster than you can blink."

Lord Rake cursed. Heather could see he was making terrible calculations in his mind.

"You would kill a defenseless doe?" Heather asked, striding to the hooded figure.

"I would," he said.

"What are you, a monster?"

"Why," he said, pushing back his hood to reveal a familiar grey face. "Don't you recognize me, girl? I'm your uncle. I am Garten Longtreader."

Heather blinked and stumbled back. This was the rabbit, her father's brother, who had betrayed King Jupiter to Morbin years before. She was stunned. A torrent of curses and accusations formed on her tongue. But before she could speak them, Bleston, Perkinson, and the rest of their Terralain force came running out of the cave, shielding their eyes.

"Ah," Bleston said, "we're all here now." He pointed at Emma. "Take her!"

His guards, led by Perkinson, ran to obey. Lord Rake fidgeted angrily. A Terralain archer moved forward and drew back his bowstring in warning. Heather stepped between Perkinson and Emma.

"Move or be moved, Heather," Perk said. "Can't you see that it's over?"

"I never will."

Heather stood her ground. Perkinson studied her a moment, then lashed out with his fist, striking her hard across the jaw. The blow sent Heather toppling to the ground. She shook her head and levered up on an elbow, blinking away tears. She heard Emma scream, saw her run at Perkinson. Emma struck out at him, but he roughly subdued her in seconds.

"Easy with my prize," Garten Longtreader said, eying Perkinson.

Heather's jaw throbbed, and she tasted blood in her mouth. She spat and rose, glowering at the collection of traitors, while Perkinson tied Emma's hands behind her back.

"You will never live down this shame, Bleston," Lord Rake said, spitting.

"But he will have a throne from which to enjoy it," Garten Longtreader said. He strolled over to take charge of Emma. "And he'll have a treaty with Lord Morbin that no war could ever hope to achieve."

"You're assuming we would lose," Heather said, subtly studying the plateau. Lord Rake's archers knelt nearby, their hands clasped behind their heads, their bows and arrows heaped in piles. The catapult crews were seated on the ground, and all were guarded by a handful of Terralain soldiers. They must have the majority of their force still out on the mountain ridge, and these few snuck in through a secret passage. No doubt they'd been led in by Perkinson.

The Terralain soldiers had their bows trained on the Cloud Mountain captains, Lord Rake, and Emma. Heather herself was so unimportant to them that she didn't even warrant a guard.

Garten laughed. "Of course you would lose! You're losing right now. Less than a mile from where we stand, your pitiful forces are being crushed."

"Because of this villainous treachery," Emma said. "Which is ever Morbin's way."

"History may tell a different tale," Garten said, rubbing his chin beneath a smirking smile. "As ever, it is written by the victors."

"We will have peace," Bleston said.

"What kind of peace? And at what price?" Lord Rake growled.

"A tolerably good peace, I think. And it comes fairly cheap," Bleston said, glancing at Emma. "It will only cost us the last drops of Jupiter's blood."

Chapter Forty-Four

THE LAST, DESPERATE THROW

Picket felt as if he were standing in a burning building, unable to move while the ceiling crashed down on him and his helpless companions. The Lords of Prey were having their way in the battle. In very little time they would shred the rabbit army to tatters. The wolves were in full fury, fighting like the mad beasts they were, tearing through the ranks of rabbits with gleeful ease.

"If we could only get to the platform on Cloud Mountain," Helmer said, "we could find out why they aren't firing their catapults!"

"If we could pin back the blasted birds for a bit," Captain Frye shouted, "we might get our army through the wolf lines and retreat up toward the ridges!" He had just joined a last-ditch council along the rocky edge of Rockback Valley, where the brave battered rabbits were making a final desperate stand in front of the last working catapult.

Another barrel launched, exploding in a bright burst above the desperate rabbits. Picket looked at the creaking catapult and frowned.

"How many more can she fire, Heyward?" Helmer asked.

"Not more than two, sir! Probably just one."

"Let's make it a good one," Helmer called. He ordered the engineers to load one last keg and crank down the arm. The braided ropes groaned as they took on the tension, and the wood seemed certain to crack and shatter, just as the others had.

"What's the best strategy here, Frye?" Helmer asked, gazing out at the ominous scene.

"It's time, I'm afraid," Captain Frye said, "to hurt them all we can before we fall."

Picket didn't need to hear those words to know it was true. He could see the end approaching. "We need to buy as much time as we can to lessen the pressure on Cloud Mountain," he said. "Maybe Emma can escape." *And please, Heather too.*

"Let's go down with that hope in our hearts!" Captain Frye said, looking each rabbit in the eye. "It's an honor to die alongside you."

They turned then, Captains Helmer and Frye, Picket Longtreader, Jo Shanks, and Cole Blackstar. Unsheathing swords, faces like thunder, they raised their arms and called out, "My place beside you! My blood for yours!"

And all the rabbits fighting desperately at the base of Cloud Mountain shouted together, "Till the Green Ember rises, or the end of the world!"

Picket's heart raced, and, taking a deep breath, he set

himself to burst onto the nearest enemy.

"Picket, wait!" Heyward shouted. "Come with me, please."

Grabbing Picket's arm, he led him to a baggage cart behind the catapult. "Put this on!" Heyward bent, unrolling a long durable cape inset with several rods. A thick long rod like a quarterstaff lay along the spine, buckled onto the cape with metal clamps. Picket was intrigued, but he glanced back eagerly at the doomed charge of his fellows.

"What is this, Heyward?" he asked as Heyward unfastened his back-scabbard and handed it to Picket. Then the blue-robed rabbit connected a sturdy belt around his waist, pressing the large rod uncomfortably into the middle of his back.

"It's our last chance."

A minute later, Picket was wearing the strange cape contraption. His sword was sheathed at his side now, and his mind was bursting with confusion and wonder, but he listened to Heyward's harried directions, climbed the catapult, and settled into the net. Arrows whizzed past him, and everywhere the desperate struggle raged on.

"Remember," Heyward called, "arms straight out to engage! Twist inside to lock the rods! Twist out to disengage! Are you ready?"

"No!"

There was a sudden ear-splitting shriek. Heyward drew his sword and, glancing at the hawk descending on them, sliced down on the rope that held the strained wooden arm back. Picket's eyes widened. The rope parted, and the giant catapult arm sprang forward, shattering as it sent Picket sailing into the sky.

Chapter Forty-Five

PICKET'S FLIGHT

Picket was flying, actually flying, now.

Arms at his sides, he sped like an arrow past the attacking hawk and into the bright blue heaven. His heart raced, terror giving way to exhilaration.

He flew up and up, through a sky littered with birds, speeding past several by a narrow margin. Looking down, he saw the battle scene shrinking beneath him. He gritted his teeth and looked ahead.

An imperious eagle. Blade naked, glinting in the sunlight. Dead ahead.

The razor-beaked raptor beat his wings, arcing to align with the path of the soaring rabbit's flight. Picket panicked, tried to swerve, but sped on, arms flailing. He gripped the handles on the edges of his cape, trying desperately to recall Heyward's hurried instructions. Then, shooting his arms out wide, he twisted his straining wrists inward.

He heard the rattling lock of linked shafts across his spine and arms, and the soft draped cape suddenly became rigid. Picket noticed the abrupt change in his position.

Wind filled the flapping fabric, which arced taut in the new tension.

Picket rose. Then, turning, he dipped and spun a moment until he regained his balance to ride an uneasy current of air. It took all his concentration to stay on top of the whipping wind. At every moment, it threatened to unsettle the delicate balance of his wings.

He and all his ancestors had been land-bound rabbits. And now he was flying. The cape had become a glider. Picket's new flight path had swept him away from the eagle. He smiled, a steady confidence growing within.

A sudden screech and whoosh derailed his exultant thoughts, sending him into a desperate effort to escape. The great bird appeared on his right, bending toward him with a practiced grace. The eagle shrieked again, swinging his slicing sword to cut him down and send Picket crashing back to earth.

Picket tried to bank, raising his right arm to ride the rising wind, but the raptor simply matched his movement with more ease, inching ever closer. He glanced at his sword, snugly fit in the sheath at his side. But his arms were locked. How could he bring his blade to bear on this agile attacker?

The eagle banked again, dreadfully close, and swung his long sword in a sweeping slash. Desperate, Picket twisted his wrists out, disengaging the linking rods, and reached for his sword as the glider's wings luffed limply in the wind. His sword came out like a spring, ripped from its sheath in a desperate snatch, and he blocked the eagle's flashing blade. The stroke rattled his wrists, sending a numb shock thundering up his arms. With his cape-glider disengaged, he fell like a stone.

The eagle shrieked and beat his wings, dropping in a sudden attack.

Snatching desperate glances up at the bird, Picket clung to his blade. Somehow, he sent out his arms again, blade now firm in his right hand. He twisted his wrists, the rods came rigid, and he felt the tightening brace of Heyward's mad contraption.

The cloth wings came taut, catching Picket in a swift rise. He swooped up toward the diving bird. The eagle had been intent on reaching a falling rabbit. He adjusted quickly to Picket's sudden upward surge.

But not quickly enough.

As the eagle drew back his long blade, Picket soared in, banking briefly to bring his own blade into his enemy's heart.

The collision rattled Picket's bones, and he was knocked back by the dying bird's last swipe. The eagle dropped as Picket fell into a flipping spin. He lost his grip on his sword hilt. Spinning wildly in midair, he saw his treasured sword falling fast. The wind beat his body. He felt himself growing dizzy.

Then he saw something below in a sudden break of the fog. He wasn't sure if it was an evil dream or a cruel trick of the sweeping mist.

Chapter Forty-Six

To the Edge and Over

Heather heard a swishing noise and looked up, alarmed. The fog came in white clumps, just now thick again. An enormous eagle broke through the sweeping mist. Falling, not flying.

Like thunder, the bird's body slammed into the edge of the platform, bursting bricks from mortar. It bounced from the low-walled edge to tumble into the rocky ravine below. There was a long fall in silence before its rough landing echoed in their ears.

This unsettled the scene on the plateau, drawing everyone's attention to the bird. Several rabbits ran to the edge to watch him plunge. Heather took a chance and rushed at Perkinson, lashing out with her feet in a kick that sent him sprawling. He dropped his sword as he tumbled back.

It fell at Lord Rake's feet. He took it up and swung down hard on the steel helm of the nearest Terralain guard. Bleston turned in time to see Emma's bonds being cut. Cursing and barking orders, he rallied his rabbits to regain control. He pointed to Emma. "Kill her!" he shouted. Then he raised his own blade and charged toward Heather.

His lieutenant turned to Emma and raised his bow, releasing a driving dart.

Many things happened at once. Lord Rake leapt through the air, placing his body between the arrow and Emma. It caught him square in the chest, and he crashed to the ground.

Emma screamed, rushing to Lord Rake's side as Heather raced to the scene. She meant to help Lord Rake, but Bleston and several of his soldiers were closing on Emma, their swords poised as they charged. Heather saw Bleston, face full of fury, the Whitson Stone bouncing beneath his chin, as the old warrior came for the princess. He was attacking his own flesh and blood, his own niece, with murder in his eyes.

Emma rose, bravely facing the assault, then flinched back as a speeding blade fell from the sky above. A sword broke the bank of fog to crash onto the stones. There was a rattling clank as something came apart, though the blade remained intact.

Heather gazed in amazement as a brilliant emerald gem on a strong slender chain rebounded into the air between Bleston and Emma.

The Green Ember.

Bleston stopped, wide-eyed, and snatched the emerald out of the air. Almost laughing, he pocketed the gem and turned back to Emma.

"Now, Princess, you die!"

Before Heather could act, something arced from the sky and smashed into Bleston. He rolled over the ground, entangled with his attacker, to the broken edge of the plateau, where they crashed and rolled apart.

Heather's mouth fell open. "Picket!" She ran to help him up.

Bleston rose slowly, turning on Picket with a fierce shout.

"Longtreader!"

Bleston was breathing hard as one of his soldiers handed him a sword. He pointed it at Picket with unguarded rage on his face. He was sweating, his fur matted and his eyes wild. The calm, composed, commanding Silver Prince was gone. He unleashed a near-lupine growl, then ran.

Picket stood firm on the plateau edge and pushed Heather away.

Emma took up Picket's sword and heaved it toward him. Picket reached for it.

But it was too late.

Bleston was on him. The older rabbit made to drive for Picket's middle, but when Picket swiveled to avoid it, Bleston brought his blade down in the two-handed hammering slice he had always intended.

It was a move Helmer often used. It would have taken Picket's head off. But he saw it just in time.

Picket dipped back, staggered, but kept his feet as the death stroke grazed his chest, sparking on his breastplate.

Bleston's momentum, only barely checked from his charging run, carried him forward, past Picket. He tripped on the shattered edge of the wall, snatching at Picket's cape as he plummeted over the edge.

Heather watched in horror as Picket was dragged over with him.

Chapter Forty-Seven

TRAITORS' DAY

Heather screamed. She and Emma leapt onto the low wall. They gazed below in terror but were arrested by a shout from behind. They turned to see Perkinson, sword drawn, a fierce scowl on his face.

"Surrender, Emma," he said. "I'll kill her!" he shouted as the Cloud Mountain company became aware of this fresh peril. They had regained the plateau from Bleston's fewer rabbits. "The first arrow I see nocked, I do the worst," he said, inching closer to Emma with his blade. There were still a few yards between them, but Heather, who was directly behind Emma, knew how quickly Perk could close that distance.

"Wait!" Heather cried, waving off the gathering soldiers. "He'll do it. He'll do it. He's a monster, and he won't hesitate. Stay back!" They heeded her warning, backing off and lowering their bows.

"Perkinson, please. My father, the one who has always cared for me," Emma said, tears starting in her eyes, "is lying over there, dying. Your master, Bleston, is dead, and

Picket—your fellow Fowler and my dear friend—with him. What could you possibly want now?"

"I want to make the trade," he said. Then louder, "I still want to make the treaty, Garten!"

As if summoned by these words, Garten Longtreader approached. The grey rabbit had been slowly withdrawing as the spectacle unfolded. But now he reemerged, smiling as he came. "The treaty still stands and can fall to Prince Kylen in his father's stead."

"Then we are agreed?" Perkinson asked.

"Yes," Garten said. "But I'd rather have her alive, if possible."

Perkinson pointed his sword at Emma, stepped closer. "I don't know how we can do that, Ambassador Longtreader."

"It's quite simple, really," Garten said, reaching into his robes to draw out a small wooden whistle. "I blow this, and my carrier comes. If I don't blow this or am not returned well and safe within the hour, then the enormous reserve force will level this place—all of Cloud Mountain—without a drop of mercy."

"So your safety is guaranteed no matter what," Perkinson said, scowling. "But mine isn't. I will die up here, and I'd like to take her with me!"

Just then, a rabbit glided up out of the ravine, sweeping over the ledge. He rose in an artful arc, flipping smoothly backward before landing on the rock between Emma and Perkinson. Picket landed cleanly, crouching with one hand on the ground, head down, his cape draped around him.

He looked up and slowly raised a sword.

Perkinson started back, gasping. Then he cried out in fury and frustration. He aimed a thunderous overhead stroke at Picket, but it was firmly, almost casually, deflected. Heather's eyes widened as she gazed at her brother. He was so sure of himself, so bold. Picket strode forward along the narrow top of the stone wall. He knocked aside another swiping slice from Perk, then three more strokes in rapid succession. Each were blocked with a furious calm, the last exposing Perkinson's middle. Picket went for it, his face grim as he sent his enemy—his former friend—over the edge.

Chapter Forty-Eight

A Deadly Deal

Picket turned, searching in fury for other enemies to be dealt with. The Cloud Mountain captains now had the remnant of Bleston's soldiers under guard, but many pointed at the lone free enemy. The robed rabbit.

"Who are you?" Picket asked.

"I'm your uncle," he said. "I'm Garten Longtreader."

"Of course you are," Picket said, spitting as he strode forward, brandishing his weapon—the sword he had wrested from Bleston as they fell. He had seen his uncle once before, at Jupiter's Crossing when the gray rabbit left Smalls for dead.

"Princess Emma," Garten said, lifting the whistle near his lips. "May I have a quiet word?"

"Picket," Emma called. "Hold on, please."

Picket turned, perplexed by her command. "Your Highness?"

"I will speak to this rabbit," she said. "But first I must see to Lord Rake." Picket watched as Emma and Heather ran to the fallen rabbit. *How did this happen? He can't be...*

Emma knelt beside Lord Rake as Heather reached for his wrist, waited, and shook her head. Emma's head dropped, and she began to weep. But with a quick breath, she settled herself. She rose and walked to where Picket hovered near the traitor, his sword extended.

Picket saw she was working hard to master her grief. She looked at Picket. "Thank you, my friend, for what you've done today. But I must speak with this rabbit a moment."

Picket frowned.

"I am unarmed," Garten said, pulling back his robes to prove he had no sword or knife. He raised the whistle again. "This is my only weapon."

"I need a few minutes," Emma said.

Picket bowed and backed away, uneasy. He went to pick up his own sword, casting Bleston's aside in disgust. Then he saw something else on the ground.

An emerald gem on a golden chain. He picked it up.

Heather came and took his arm, laying her head on his shoulder. Picket fought back tears. It had all happened so fast. Perkinson! His heart ached. Before that the fall, the fight with Bleston. Bleston carrying him over the edge. His horrid mid-fall tussle with Bleston, until he finally broke free with his enemy's sword, engaging his cape-glider at the last moment. As the rods clicked in place, so did his mind. He finally understood how the invention worked. Heyward was a genius to design such a thing.

When Heyward's face came into his mind, he jumped suddenly forward, alarming Heather.

"The catapults!" he cried, racing to the stunned captains who had watched the drama unfold. "Send everything you've got! Now! Our fighters are backed up against the far edge of Rockback Valley, and they desperately need relief!"

"Shall we send a company to reinforce, Lieutenant?" one of the catapult captains asked.

"Yes!" Picket cried. "Send whoever can be spared. Our forces are pinned against the rock wall. Light up the sky!" he shouted at the soldiers cranking down the arms. "And, archers! Move down the mountain where you can get a clean shot at them!"

Runners were dispatched, and nearly all the attendant archers were sent through the tunnels down to the field.

Would they arrive in time? Picket hoped so. The catapults leapt forward, sending their blastpowder kegs aloft. Explosions followed as the shattered barrels broke open the sky. Orange and red tongues of fire stretched across the horizon as the fog mixed with a sudden rising smoke.

Seeing he could do little to help the catapult crews, he returned to stand beside Heather. Emma emerged from her short conference with their uncle.

The old rabbit—bearing such a woeful resemblance to their father and Uncle Wilfred—smiled as they walked near.

"He is to be allowed to leave," Emma said, a stern sadness in her eyes.

"Your Highness?" Picket asked, aghast. "Hasn't he orchestrated this betrayal, along with Bleston and Perk?"

"He is to be allowed to go," she repeated. "Let Garten Longtreader go to the seventh standing stone."

"But Emma," Heather whispered, "we don't understand."

A grumbling arose among the captains and lieutenants. "Your Highness," the archer captain said. "They've killed our Lord Rake. How can you let him go?"

"Am I the heir of King Jupiter?" Emma asked, her voice even, her fists clenched, and her back straight. "Do I command here, or not?"

Heads down, they made no reply.

"You are and you do, Your Highness," Picket said. He looked around, as if challenging any of them to object. He knelt wearily on one knee. "What you command, we will do."

The other soldiers followed Picket's example, kneeling before Emma. Heather knelt beside her friend, her brow knit in concern.

With a flick of his chin, Picket motioned for his uncle to move on. The grey rabbit blew his whistle, then smiled and bowed briefly. He turned to Emma, extending his hand. "So we have an agreement, Princess?"

"We do," she said, shaking Garten's hand and then stuffing her fists into her pockets.

Garten nodded, then made his way along the wall's edge until he came to the standing stones. He ran up the winding stones steps that wrapped around the last, and looking around proudly as if he'd won a great victory, he laughed. In a few moments a bird swooped down from above the seven standing stones. Beating his wings, he hovered beside him. Garten leapt onto his back-saddle and flew into the sky, away from the blasts of the catapults and the tumult of battle.

"Now what?" Heather asked.

Emma sighed. "The force attacking our soldiers below is only half of Morbin's army. If Garten had not been allowed to leave, the rest would have attacked here."

"Why won't they now?" Picket asked.

"They had a deal with Bleston," Emma said, looking into the distance. "Now Garten says he will return to Morbin and see if the treaty they made can be extended."

"We cannot make a treaty with Morbin," Heather said, horror creeping into her expression.

"No," Emma said, "but we need to survive the next twenty-four hours."

"I don't understand," Picket said, rubbing his head.

"You don't need to understand," Emma answered, looking around. "We have work to do. Heather and I need to help with the wounded, and you, Picket," she said, motioning to the active rabbits all around the plateau, "must take Lord Rake's place and command Cloud Mountain's forces."

"Surely Captain Pacer is better suited," Picket began.

"No one can find Pacer," she answered.

"But, Your Highness," he came closer. "Emma, I'm only a lieutenant."

"You're a captain now, Shuffler," she said wearily. "You flew through the air, Picket. Actually flew. All these soldiers

saw it. You fought the Silver Prince and came out on top—
same with Perkinson. I think you can handle this."

"I will do my best, Your Highness," he said, falling to
one knee.

Emma reached out and touched his head gently, then
turned and hurried toward the caves, with Heather running
beside her.

Chapter Forty-Nine

A PLEDGE

Picket's body was exhausted, but his mind came alive as he focused all his intelligence on serving Emma as she had asked. He organized the scattered captains, assigned new duties based on the changing circumstances of the battle, and sent every kind of reinforcement possible to relieve the desperate soldiers on the field below. This left Cloud Mountain badly exposed to the second half of Morbin's army, encamped on the other side of the mountain. But there was nothing else to be done.

Somehow Emma trusted Garten Longtreader to deliver a temporary peace, and Picket fought back a chorus of objections as he went about his work. His present concerns were enough to keep him occupied. The rest would have to wait. He had to trust the princess. He had to trust his friend.

The tide had turned in the Battle of Rockback Valley. The catapult bombardment from above, along with the fresh rabbits pouring into the valley from the heights of Cloud Mountain, meant the bedraggled rabbits could last the day. Though hundreds fell in the battle, many more survived, and by the dying light they made their weary way into the stronghold of Cloud Mountain.

"I'm ever so glad to see you, son," Helmer said, clasping Picket in an embrace. Helmer looked awful, wounded and limping, but he was smiling. "I'm told that you organized the reinforcements—that you saved us."

"He saved more than you," Emma said, crossing to examine this last batch of returning soldiers. Almost all were wounded, and many carried unconscious comrades. "But let's save the medals for later. Right now I need the worst of the wounded over there," she pointed, raising her voice. "And those with minor injuries, here. If you're not certain, then go with the more severe. Knowing this lot, I'm sure you're more likely to underestimate your injuries." Emma moved away, directing the groups and seeing to the most urgent needs. "Bring more boiled water and call for Doctor Zeiger," she shouted, and she disappeared into her surgery tent.

"Where's Captain Frye?" Heather asked, and Picket could see she was worried. He was too. "And Heyward?" she continued, casting about for them, "Please don't tell me—"

"The dead. They're seeing to the dead, Heather," Captain Helmer said. "Both came out well enough."

Heather sighed, smiled, then turned and followed Emma into the tent.

"And the enemy?" Picket asked. "Have they fallen back to rejoin the others?"

"They fell back," Helmer said, "but I don't know about joining the others. What others?"

"There's another army out there," Picket said.

"Bleston's forces?"

"Well, yes. I suppose Kyle has command of those, and we don't know where they are. But Morbin's got another army out there, as big again as the one we fought today. I sent scouts to confirm it, sir." He explained Bleston's treacherous treaty with the king of the Lords of Prey and Emma's improvised bargain with Garten Longtreader.

"She can't really trust him, can she?" Helmer asked.

"I have my doubts, Captain. But so far they haven't attacked. And why not? They could have crushed us in here."

"Likely, yes," Helmer said, slumping into an offered chair. "But this place really is a fortress. It's easy to slip small groups in here if you know the ways, but it's blasted hard to overcome with large numbers in a direct assault. Still," he said, shaking his head, "if they have another army that size, they could almost certainly do it."

"But they'd risk losing a second battle," Picket said, "or at least not winning a second."

"A very small risk."

"Maybe it's not a risk Morbin's willing to take."

"Perhaps you're right," Helmer mused, "but I'm uneasy about this bargain the princess made."

"I trust her," Picket said, frowning. "But I'm worried too. Right now Emma needs our support, perhaps more than anything else. The community has to rally behind her."

Helmer nodded.

Captain Frye entered the great hall, flanked by a bleary-eyed Heyward in his tattered blue robe. Picket knew their duty with the deceased must have been grim, but he crossed to Heyward and embraced him.

"You did it, Heyward," Picket said. "They will call me a hero, say I saved the day, but I will never forget that it was you. Thank you, hero Heyward, my dear friend."

* * *

Heather worked hard, pushing past the insistent fatigue that threatened to overwhelm her. For the past several hours she had been like an extra pair of hands for Emma, assisting the princess in delicate surgeries and simple stitches.

At last she and Emma were free of their most urgent cases. She followed Emma and removed her blood-stained apron, laying it aside, and bent to wash in a fresh basin of hot water.

"I think we may rest a little," Emma said, slumping into a chair on the inside edge of the tent. "But I'll need to see to things outside soon."

"Surely they don't need you now," Heather said. She stood, stretched her arms, and moved toward the fabric door. When she looked outside, she gasped.

"What is it?" Emma asked, getting to her feet. Heather motioned for her to follow and left the tent.

More than a thousand rabbits, in row upon row, stood quietly at attention facing the small surgical tent. The medical center was still in motion, with doctors and volunteers buzzing around, checking on patients. But the ranks of rabbits were silent. When Emma emerged, her hand went over her mouth.

Captain Frye called out, "Attention!"

The rabbits stepped in unison, bringing their heels together, placing their fists over their hearts.

"Your Highness," Picket said, moving forward, a wooden box in his hands.

"Captain Longtreader?"

"We know you are tired and that we all need rest. But we have gathered the army, at least those soldiers well enough to stand, so that we may pledge ourselves to you."

Emma stood tall, walked forward to the front of the makeshift assembly, and nodded gratefully to the gathered soldiers. Heather marveled at her poise, especially after so trying a day. She had learned her true identity, learned that she had lost her brother, and had been put in charge of an army—a movement. And she had been betrayed, had become the object of an attempted capture, nearly killed. She had lost the only father she had ever known in Lord Rake. She had worked for hours performing surgeries. But Heather saw no sign of vulnerability in Emma as she strode to the front of this company. Her back was straight and her head high. Tears welled in her eyes, but she made no move to wipe them away.

"You have done your community and our cause a great service today," she said to the assembly of soldiers. "I'm so proud of you. Please, keep on fighting for this cause, no matter what happens. My father…" she paused to collect herself. "Lord Rake, our guiding star for so many years, gave his life today for this cause. My brother, Prince Smalden Joveson, or Jupiter Smalls as he was known here, gave his life for us all. And not just in the end. All his life he worked for the Mended Wood. I can promise you that I will do the same. To honor Lord Rake, I will give all I have. I will give my life, in honor of the fallen prince and our father and the great cause for which we all fight."

Even the medical area was silent now, every rabbit hanging on Emma's words. "Thank you, brave soldiers. Today you struck a blow that echoes in Morbin's secret keep and rings in his ears. Today, you learned your prince was dead, but you battled on without him. Battle on, friends, whatever comes."

She looked at Heather, grief threatening to overwhelm her. But she hardened her face again, turning to the assembly. "Battle on, brothers!" she shouted, and the soldiers raised an exuberant cheer. "For Jupiter's cause!" she cried. Another joyful cheer.

Her voice grew quieter, and such a hush fell that everyone heard her words clearly. "For the Mended Wood and the whole wounded world. Bear the flame."

Quiet applause began and quickly built, mixed with rising cheers, until the room trembled with the tumult of voices and the swelling thunderous applause.

A Pledge

When the cheering quieted to a gentle roar, Picket moved toward Emma. He motioned for Heather to come beside him and handed Heather the box. Opening it, he drew out the Green Ember, and to the frenzied cheers of the company, he settled the chain around Emma's neck.

Captain Frye and Helmer, aided by stout soldiers, brought a platform and set it beside Emma. The old captains took her hands and led her to the elevated stage. She stood in view of the whole assembly, the bright emerald glinting in the torchlight. The captains saluted her, then bowed low, before backing away.

After more cheers, the room settled down, a low murmur of awed exultations fading into silence.

Picket spoke. "Your Highness, hear our pledge!"

With clenched fists over their hearts and tears in many eyes, the assembled soldiers called out to their princess, "My place beside you, my blood for yours! Till the Green Ember rises, or the end of the world!"

More cheers followed, and Heather watched her friend in awe. The princess stood firm, a tower they all turned to in their desperate battle for hope. Heather understood what Emma meant to them all, even if Emma didn't yet know it herself.

Chapter Fifty

THE DARKNESS BEFORE DAWN

Heather woke in the middle of the night. She had fallen asleep with a kind of happiness in her heart. Now the feeling was replaced by a welling dread. Picket slept heavily nearby, fresh from his duty on the first watch. She decided not to wake him. She rose and dressed, lit a candle, slung on her satchel, and left the room.

She started to make for Emma's room in Lord Rake's quarters but found herself moving in another direction. She passed through Hallway Round and out into a frosty fog-thick night. She peered into the blinding mist as she walked carefully on, seeing many weary soldiers gathered around a low blaze in the midst of the village green. Bypassing them, she made her way toward the caves, fear throbbing in her heart.

In minutes she had emerged on the other side of the caves, onto the staging plateau. It was thick with heavy, haunting fog. Her candle was little help, but she made her way carefully to the edge and felt for the bottom of one of the catapults. They had been moved to the other side of the ground, aimed at the next threat, since Rockback Valley was empty of battle.

Climbing the catapult, she broke through the bank of fog and hung on, suspended over the plateau. What she saw in the moonlight confirmed her worst fears.

The tops of the seven standing stones peeked through the fog. On the last stone, a solitary rabbit emerged and stood, stretching her torch aloft. She held something small in her hand. Heather remembered the whistle her uncle had used to summon his bird and how after he had used it, he shook Emma's hand.

"Emma!" she cried, her throat tight. "Emma, no!" She saw no movement atop the stone, so she hurried down the catapult, missing handholds, falling the last several feet, and losing her candle. Forgetting the peril of the plateau edge and nearly blind in the dense mist, Heather ran toward the standing stones, her hands stretched out before her.

At last her hands found the solid rock. She wasn't sure which stone it was, but it was likely the first or second. She moved on, hurrying, feeling her way past five more stones. She ran up the winding steps and emerged from the mist to discover that she was on the sixth stone. Emma was many yards away on the seventh.

"Emma!" she cried. "You must not do this."

The princess turned, her face sad but settled. "My dear Heather, there is nothing else I can do."

"You can live. And fight," Heather said, her voice breaking.

"This is my way of fighting."

"No, Emma. No!"

"Go back, Heather. Leave me to do what I must."

"You must not surrender yourself. You cannot!"

"I can lay down what is mine," Emma said.

Heather frowned. "You sound like Bleston. The queenship you'll have—your inheritance—it's not your own property. It's not something you can trade or give away as you see fit. It's a duty, a calling, not a possession!"

"So I may order countless rabbits to their deaths—defending and protecting *me*—but I may not lay my own life down?"

"Not like this," Heather said. "No, my dear, not like this. You may not. Even royal heirs must know their limits."

"But Heather, it's settled," Emma said, emotion choking her words. "If I'm not here to be carried off when Garten's bird comes, they will turn this place to rubble. Everyone will be killed! I'm not a fool, Heather. They can do it, and they will."

"But if you're gone, what hope do we have?"

"You'll carry on, Heather. You'll find a way to continue the struggle. You'll survive."

"Emma, you're wrong. You are the last link we have to our hope. If you are gone, then the cause is truly lost. The Mended Wood is ended in our hearts. We may survive—may remain alive—but how many of those who swore to die for you tonight would choose a life of cowering in a world without hope? I do not choose that. Please don't make this choice for us all."

"There's no right way now," Emma said, raising the whistle to her lips. "It's all darkness and mist."

"Don't, Emma!" Heather cried.

The princess blew a long, shrill note on the whistle. Heather's heart sank and she staggered back, as if hit with a killing blow. A shriek pierced the night air.

"It's a good thing, Heather," Emma said. "I want you to see that I choose this. It's not a bad way to end."

"Don't do this, Emma!"

"It's done, my dear." A banking wingtip split the pale mist. Emma raised her torch high. "You bear the flame in your way," she said, "and I'll bear it in mine."

Another shriek. Closer. Closer.

Heather felt a cold weight fall on her, like early ice on an autumn garden. This all felt so wrong. She gazed at her friend, illuminated in torchlight, bravely resigned to her grim agreement. Behind her the great bird broke the bank of fog, beat his wings once and banked again, disappearing once more into the endless mist. Again his feathered wingtips cut the fog in a wispy furrow.

"It's all right, Heather," Emma said, a brave smile on her face. "I know how I'm going to die."

"I don't know how I'm going to die," Heather said, backing to the far side of the sixth standing stone, "but I know how I'm going to live."

Heather burst into a run—four stabbing strides—and then she leapt, covering the distance between the standing stones.

She landed, found her feet, and surged forward. The hawk began to emerge from the mist again. Heather shoved Emma hard, clutching the emerald at her neck. The princess fell backward, disappearing with a shocked scream into the fog below.

Heather bent to recover the fallen torch. She raised it high. In her other hand she held the Green Ember.

With a shriek, the hawk extended his talons.

* * *

Picket felt Heather's absence and came awake with a jolt. After a short search, ranging through the cold halls and foggy fields, he found Emma at the base of the seventh stone. She was hurt but stood upright, sobbing and muttering.

"Carried off!" she said. "It was meant to be me!"

Picket's heart sank. He didn't have to ask who had been carried off. He knew.

He ran up the steps and stood on the seventh stone. Emma hobbled up to stand beside him. They searched the sky for any sign of her. Finally they saw, black against the moon, a silhouette that filled their hearts with woe.

Picket stood beside Emma as they stared into the sky, watching with heavy hearts in the darkness before dawn.

Chapter Fifty-One

A BAD DREAM

Heather stood in Morbin's lair, aching and exhausted. She had been bustled into this topmost tower of the haunting High Bleaks after many cold miles in the raptor's claws. Now Morbin stared down at her from his awful throne of golden bones. Another raptor stood beside him, a brown falcon with yellow eyes. Heather had nothing but the clothes on her back and her satchel. Inside her satchel, tucked away beside a bottle in a battered old purse, lay a torch charm and an emerald gem.

"More light," Morbin demanded, his voice full of bile.

Soon more torches were lit by three hurrying rabbits— slaves, she assumed—as the massive hawk gazed at her intently. He shook his head.

Heather thought he was puzzled, perhaps even perplexed. *He should be.* The longer her true identity remained undiscovered, the more time her friends had to act. *Maybe*, she thought, *just maybe they can get out of Cloud Mountain in time.* Her hopes for her friends lay in that, but still their chances were slim. She didn't regret what she had done. But she knew that the whole endeavor rested on the edge of a knife. Her hope was faint.

Staring around at Morbin's awful lair, his grotesque throne, at the wordless slaves obeying him, what small hope she had was ebbing away.

"Will Ambassador Longtreader ever come?" Morbin demanded.

"He was sent for, Lord Morbin," the falcon said. He screeched a call that brought an old red rabbit scurrying through black double doors.

"Where is Garten?" the falcon asked.

"Lord Shelt," the red rabbit said, bowing low, "we have sent Marbole, and Ambassador Longtreader should arrive at any moment."

Morbin screeched a curse, knocking down the plate and glass that had been set by his throne. "If he's not here soon, Slave Gritch, I will execute every rabbit slave in this place."

"Yes, King Morbin," Gritch said, backing away.

"Gather them all!" Morbin shouted. "Every rabbit in the palace, gather them outside the door! If he isn't here soon, I'll start with you, Gritch."

"Yes, lord," Gritch said, tripping through the doorway. Heather heard shouts and scattered footfalls outside. She clenched her jaws.

"Who are you?" Morbin asked, his eyes narrowing. "Are you her? Are you my old enemy's heir?"

Heather said nothing.

"Even if he doesn't come to identify you, I can find out," Morbin said, glancing at his long black sickle. "I can ask him who you *were*."

There was a commotion outside, and the door opened. Garten Longtreader stumbled in, and Heather glanced through the doorway to see silhouettes of several rabbit slaves gathered in the hallway.

"Where have you been?" Morbin snapped.

"I beg pardon, Lord Morbin," Garten said.

"Is this her? Is it the princess?"

Heather tried to turn away, but he saw at once who she was.

"No, Lord Morbin," he said. "It is not her."

Morbin flashed out a talon, latching on to his sickle. Heather's heart raced as the black bird brought the deadly weapon down with incredible speed and force onto the table that had held his toppled tray. The wooden table parted cleanly as Morbin's blade sunk into the stone floor.

"You know who she is, don't you, Garten?" Shelt asked.

"I do. Lord Morbin, this is Heather Longtreader, my niece."

"Your niece?"

"Yes, my king."

"Then we should simply kill her now," he said.

Heather heard a gasp from the hallway, but she focused on Morbin. This might be the end of her story, but she didn't want to let him see her fear. She would not grovel.

"She is, however," Garten began delicately, "something

327

of an important figure in their movement. She is called the Scribe of the Cause and has long been a favorite of Jupiter's son and daughter."

"She is, is she?" Morbin asked, his voice eerily calm.

"All the more reason to kill her," Shelt said.

"On the contrary, my lord. She may be a valuable pawn," Garten offered.

"Maybe we should bury her with that blundering little prince," Morbin said. "Perhaps they belong in that tomb together."

Heather squinted against unbidden tears. She didn't want to show her pain, but her heart broke when he spoke of Smalls.

"What do we do about the princess, lord?" Garten asked. "Emma defied us by sending this rabbit in her place. She has broken our pact and now schemes against you in blatant defiance."

"She meant to keep your pact," Heather said, her voice sounding strange in this place, "though I can't imagine why she trusted you. I prevented her and took her place."

A silence followed. Morbin stared at her, his head cocked to one side, then the other. "You think yourself heroic?" he asked at last.

"I think myself a simple rabbit," she said, "loyal to the true heir and contemptuous of all traitors and dictator slavers."

Morbin laughed, then loosed a long, furious screech. He lurched forward, lashing out with his talon, knocking

Heather backward across the floor and into the far wall. A scream filled the hallway.

"Convene my war council!" Morbin growled at Shelt, "I will accept no more excuses. This rabble must be routed!" The beastly bird beat his black wings and swooped out the hangar on the far side of his lair.

Heather rose slowly to her feet, agonizing pain erupting in her side and left leg.

"Ambassador, make preparations for the war council to meet," Shelt said. "Many will still be in the field, and I have word that General Flox fell in the battle. Find the highest ranking wolf and get him here."

"Yes, lord. And what are your orders concerning her?" Garten asked, pointing to Heather.

"Lord Morbin said we ought to bury her with Jupiter Smalls, did he not?"

"He said we might," Garten said, "but we might just as well keep her to use against the heir."

"Either way, she has no hope," Shelt said.

"Of course not," Garten agreed. "There is no hope for her side in this war. I realized that years ago."

"You chose well," Shelt said. "Perhaps this rabbit girl will follow her uncle's example."

"Never," Heather said. She would never let them see her surrender, and nothing would ever induce her to turn traitor. But her heart was very low. She was exhausted and in great pain. She was helpless, trapped in the lair of their greatest enemy. She had little reason to hope and every excuse to despair.

Then she heard something. Soft words in the distance. No, not just words. A song.

> *"The skies once so blue and beautiful,*
> *Are littered with crass, cruel foes.*
> *Their bleak, black wings beat a dreadful beat,*
> *Over sorrowful songs of woes."*

The song rose, and the words rang clearer.

"Who is that?" Shelt shouted. "Is that a *slave?*"

"I don't know, Lord Shelt," Garten said, though Heather could see the fear in his eyes.

> *"Songs of suffering and cruel murders,*
> *All lament and never a voice,*
> *Raised in grateful gladness to the heights,*
> *Never reason to rejoice."*

"Who is singing?" Shelt cried, screeching a curse. "Find that rabbit and kill her!"

Garten nodded, bowed clumsily, and disappeared through the doorway as Shelt fumed. Heather began to smile, even as tears stood out in her eyes. It was an old, familiar song.

> *"But, it will not be so in the Mended Wood,*
> *We'll be free and glad again.*
> *It will not be so in the Mended Wood,*

When the heir of Jupiter reigns.
When the heir of Jupiter reigns!"

Heather knew the song, yes. But she knew more than that. She knew exactly who was singing. Her heart flooded with a sudden, surging hope.

The End

Keep up with author
S. D. Smith

Sign up for his funny, infrequent newsletter for
good deals, news about upcoming books, and more.

www.sdsmith.net/updates

*If you loved the book, please give it a review online
now. Positive reviews help so much. Thank you.*

Don't miss the other books in this series.

The Green Ember

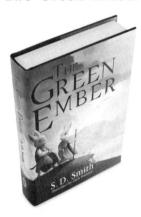

and its prequel,
The Black Star of Kingston